"I love this dress," Jason murmured.

"I'd love it even better if it was lying on the grass. I can't go another day, another night without you, Liv. Let me love you, as I want to. Don't be sad and bitter. I've been punished."

Olivia was very near tears. "What are you saying, Jason? You want us to start over?"

"Yes!" His tone was urgent, heartfelt. "Haven't we both suffered enough? I want you back, Liv."

Margaret Way takes great pleasure in her work and works hard at her pleasure. She enjoys tearing off to the beach with her family at weekends, loves haunting galleries and auctions and is completely given over to French champagne "for every possible joyous occasion." She was born and educated in the river city of Brisbane, Australia, and now lives within sight and sound of beautiful Moreton Bay.

Books by Margaret Way

HARLEQUIN ROMANCE®
3767—RUNAWAY WIFE*
3771—OUTBACK BRIDEGROOM*
3775—OUTBACK SURRENDER*
3803—INNOCENT MISTRESS

HARLEQUIN SUPERROMANCE®
1111—SARAH'S BABY*
1183—HOME TO EDEN *

*Koomera Crossing

His Heiress Wife

Margaret Way

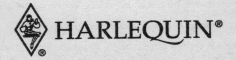

TORONTO • NEW YORK • LONDON
AMSTERDAM • PARIS • SYDNEY • HAMBURG
STOCKHOLM • ATHENS • TOKYO • MILAN • MADRID
PRAGUE • WARSAW • BUDAPEST • AUCKLAND

ISBN 0-373-03811-9

HIS HEIRESS WIFE

First North American Publication 2004.

CHAPTER ONE

ON THAT hot November afternoon before school broke up for the Christmas vacation Olivia returned to her trendy inner-city apartment to find the red light flashing on her answering machine. She pushed the button leaning casually against the kitchen counter to listen to her messages. While she was waiting she kicked off her shoes, contemplating a swim in the apartment complex's pool to relax and wind-down. She gave her attention to the mail, sorting through it quickly. She was so looking forward to the long summer break. In many ways it had been an exhausting year. Adolescent girls weren't the easiest people in the world to deal with. especially the ones who had embarked on sex lives.

There was a postcard from a friend who was always dashing off to exotic parts of the world—this time Peru, hence the picture of the ruins of Machu Picchu; a stack of invitations to Christmas functions and parties, the phone bill—accompanied by a booklet of helpful hints; a letter from a favoured charity that specialized in looking after families in need thanking her for her generous Christmas donation. She was pleased to help in fact she felt duty bound. Her career as a secondary school teacher was flourishing. She had slipped into prestigious Ormiston Girls Grammar three years earlier as though the job had been tailor made for her. She was well paid and she had private means. Why shouldn't she give something back to the community? She'd sent off cheques to other charities as well.

The first recorded message was from Matt Edwards who she had been seeing quite a bit. Matt wanted to know if she'd fancy a romantic weekend at the glorious beach resort of Noosa on the Sunshine Coast. She'd have to think about that one. She enjoyed Matt's company. He was an interesting man, but alas not rivetting. Rivetting men were few and far between which was just as well for the protection of women—such men became dangerous in the blink of an eye. Olivia thought it better to settle for quiet, everlasting devotion.

Matt was attractive with a dry sense of humour that appealed to her. He was getting to make quite a name for himself as a corporate lawyer. He'd just bought himself an expensive new car which miracle of miracles he'd allowed her to take for a short drive around the block. One would have to look really hard to find a man who appreciated a woman's driving skills let alone her intelligence, but then Matt was devoting a lot of his energies to winning Olivia over with a view to getting her to the altar. The sad part was, he wasn't succeeding. She already knew she would never love him.

She knew all about love—the sort of love that enraptured or ruined. It was Heaven or Hell and there seemed to be no in-between. Attraction was too tame after that. Any day now she would have to tell Matt he was wasting precious time. She just couldn't commit. Maybe it all stemmed from the fact that once she'd almost been married. Sometimes when she was tired or depressed and slipped unwillingly into memory she thought she might always be on her own. She'd taken scissors to her wedding dress and veil and a week later she'd cut off her long mane. No man would slide his fingers through her hair again.

"Liv, you push the guys away!" That was her friend, Julie talking. Julie tended to nag her. The thing was it wasn't easy to forget what love was like—even when love was done.

The second message was from the mother of a really problematic kid in her Maths class who'd made flouncing out of lessons an art form. Olivia hadn't been prepared to tolerate that. A grateful mother thanked her for achieving "wonderful results with Charlotte"; the third from a recently married colleague inviting her and Matt over to a dinner party—"I'm getting in early, kiddo! You're amazingly popular."

The last message profoundly shocked her. The letter opener fell out of her nerveless hand, clattering onto the tiles. Olivia moved with urgency nearer the machine, her heart lurching in anticipation of the bad news she knew instinctively was to come.

The voice was as familiar as her own but it was not the good-natured affectionate ramble she was used to. Instead Grace Gordon, Harry's long-time housekeeper, sounded wildly upset. The words came tumbling out so fast Olivia had difficulty making out exactly what Grace was saying.

"Livvy, it's me. It's Gracie, love." The voice invaded the small kitchen so loudly, it reverberated down the galley. "Livvy, you have to come home."

Olivia squeezed her eyes shut. What was wrong? It struck her immediately that it must be Harry. Harry always kept good health, but he was well into his seventies.

"Something awful has happened." The words crackled down the line. "I couldn't get through to you at the school. Some awful woman—so rude—told me you were in a meeting with the Head and couldn't be disturbed. I hate to be the bearer of sad news, love." There was a pause, as Grace battled her choking sobs, "It's your uncle Harry," she wailed, confirming Olivia's worst fears. "He's had a massive heart attack. He's dead, Livvy! Three o'clock this afternoon just when I had a nice cup of tea ready for him. It was a terrible shock—it came right out of the blue. He'd been right as rain. Jason has been wonderful. A tower of strength."

Jason? For an instant Olivia felt slashed open. How many Jasons could there be? The name struck another frightful blow. Olivia reeled back against the granite-topped counter, putting a hand over her thudding heart. What was Jason doing at Havilah? He had no right to show his face there ever again!

"Come home, love," Grace was imploring, unable to gain control of her sobs. "Jason understands you'll want to make the arrangements. Please ring me back, love, as soon as you can. I'm sorry I'm not making much sense, but I'm so upset."

And what of me? In a daze, Olivia found her way into the living room, leaving her mail to spill unregarded to the kitchen floor. She slumped into a chair, feeling as though she had been utterly gutted. Harry was dead. Jason was a tower of strength. There was something very strange indeed going on. How and why was Jason at Havilah? Wasn't Jason managing an Outback cattle station, his wife and child with him? Clearly he'd come back. But why? More importantly why hadn't Harry told her?

Because he knew how much talk of Jason would upset you, her inner voice told her. Jason Corey had caused her tremendous pain. Years before as a girl of twenty she had thought her life was over when her fiancé Jason had jilted her on the eve of their wedding. At nearly twenty-seven she imagined she'd fought free of the pain and humiliation. Yet it only took the sound of his name to undo her. Grief and bitterness ran down Olivia's cheeks in salty tears.

"Jason has been a tower of strength."

Even the way Grace said it—Grace had always had such a soft spot for Jason—told Olivia it had to be her Jason.

Her Jason? She felt a stab of self-contempt that even under the terrible stress of the moment she could revert to thinking of him that way. He'd never been hers. Even when he'd been passionately declaring his love for her he'd slept with another girl—made her pregnant. She had trusted Jason with her life and she had never forgiven him. Just as she had never forgiven Megan Duffy who had been a childhood friend and was to be one of her four chosen bridesmaids. She was Megan Corey now—Jason's wife, mother of their child. Probably there were other children, too, Jason was so bloody potent. No one would tell Olivia. Everyone realized she didn't want to know. As far as she was concerned, Jason and Megan belonged to the traumatic past. Consequently she was unwilling to believe Harry could allow Jason back into his life. When she suffered, Harry had suffered. Her uncle Harry, great-uncle really, was from her father's side of the family. He had raised her since her parents had been killed in a rail disaster when she was ten. Harry was a bachelor—no-one including Harry quite knew why—and he had inherited the family ancestral home, Havilah Plantation in tropical North Queensland. The Linfields were pioneers of the sugar industry with the great bulk of the nation's production contributed by the tropical North. In the early days Havilah had played host to Captain Louis Hope, revered as the father of the sugar industry. Born in Scotland, Captain Hope had established the first sugar cane plantation just outside Brisbane in the early 1860s. From those beginnings had grown an industry that each year traded forty million tonnes of high quality raw sugar on the world market. The Linfields had always been very proud of their heritage.

Her parents, when they had made their wills, had named Harry as her guardian should anything happen to them. In those days it was thought to be a sensible precaution. Her parents were always described as "the glamorous young Linfields." They were rich and blessed with good looks. They bore their name proudly and fully intended to live to a ripe old age.

It wasn't in their stars. Death had presented itself twelve years into an idyllic marriage when they were both still in their thirties. Death didn't miss rich families any more than it missed the poor. Three sons of the family had lost their lives fighting for the Allied cause in two World Wars.

Olivia could scarcely believe it was less than a week since she had last spoken to Harry. Sometimes she called him several times in the one week, especially as he was getting older, but with end of year activities at the school she'd been particularly busy. Sometimes she thought she desperately needed to see Havilah again, but she knew she couldn't endure it. There were too many memories to relive. She had grown tired of anguish. Her wedding reception was to have been held in Havilah's great barn, Harry had had transformed into the most marvellous banquet hall and ballroom with a springy pine floor. Every last detail had been planned to perfection. Harry had spared no expense, everyone had been so happy the very air was sweet. This was a match made in heaven. She had thought at times she couldn't possibly contain such happiness. She adored Jason. She couldn't get through a day without him. She was on fire for him. And he for her.

All lies. Jason, the very image of true love to her, had had feet of clay.

Now her beloved Harry who knew all her traumas and her triumphs had left her. She thought how wonderful he had always been to her, involving himself in every aspect of her life. She'd received an excellent education graduating from university with a degree in education by the time she was twenty. She'd confidently expected to gain a position with one of the district's high schools for a few years until she and Jason started a family. Afterwards when their much hoped for children were old enough she could resume her career.

Daydreams! But how could she have known differently? Everyone around her was convinced Jason was deeply, madly, irrevocably in love with her. His eyes when he looked at her! His voice when he spoke to her!

"He adores you!" Or so people told her.

How ghastly it had been to discover overnight that Jason had gone ahead and started a family with Megan Duffy. For a quiet girl Megan had been a fast worker. It was just as they said: still waters run deep. Megan's father and brother had worked and probably still did for Uncle Harry at the mill. When other mills had been forced to close down, Linfield had remained open and Uncle Harry had been kindness itself to the families of his employees. How Megan had repaid him. Even Megan's parents had been shockingly upset when they found out their only daughter was pregnant by Jason Corey of all people. That was some piece of information! It had shocked the entire district. Jason Corey was about to marry Olivia Linfield. Everyone knew Olivia and Jason had been bonded from childhood, they were meant for each other.

It wouldn't be the first time in life certainties didn't work out. Olivia had known that terrible day when Jason had come to her with his shattering news that could never bring herself to see him again. As soon as she was able she had moved nearly a thousand miles away to the State capital, Brisbane, enrolling for postgraduate studies so she could obtain her master's. Study was the answer. Hard work. Delivering assignments right on time. It had been a constant battle for her but she had pushed herself along, fixing her mind on a goal.

She had never gone home, Uncle Harry had always come to visit her instead. On those occasions she did everything in her power to make sure he had a lovely time. Neither of them, of course, ever mentioned Jason—that would have spoilt everything. Jason had left her life in ruins. For a long time she had hated him with her every breath, but hatred was too extreme. She had to relinquish it for acceptance. She had taken the philosophical view—it had helped her in her struggle to fight back. Now with Harry dead a great deal more courage was required of her. She would have to go home.

A sense of deep nostalgia assailed her. She saw Harry in her mind's eye. She felt his love all around her. A pulse in her temple throbbed as an image of Jason forced its way into her consciousness. The sun on his wonderful hair, a rich auburn, like a red setter's coat, the impossibly deep, bold blue of his eyes, the surprise of his olive skin that unlike most redheads took on a golden tan. That was a legacy from his Italian grandmother, Renata. So was the laughter and daring in his nature, his love of the earth, his attitude to food and wine, to art, his capacity for passion. For her Jason Corey would always define the word "lover." That was her tragedy. A lasting punishment when she had done no wrong. She was the victim, the one who had been betrayed.

As she continued to sit very quietly, her heart contracting and expanding with grief Olivia was faced with the thought that she was Harry's heir. She had known that for many years. She was in his own words, "the daughter of my heart." Now the tears started. How often had he told her that, or praised her with it in company? Havilah was hers. The realization carried enormous responsibility and enormous change. She was the only one bearing the family name left. There was extended family, of course—offspring of the daughters of the family—but she was the only Linfield. Havilah was the ancestral home, the Big House to what was once the largest and most prosperous sugar plantation in the North. When she was growing up, the sugar had been a major contributor to the nation's economy. Directly or indirectly hundreds of thousands of people had depended on it for their livelihood, but various factors contributed to falling world prices and a downturn in the industry. Planters who had long enjoyed an enviable prosperity had had to learn to diversify to survive.

Havilah had led the way.

Before Jason had betrayed her and she'd been forced to leave home she had always taken the greatest interest in Harry's wide business portfolio. He had encouraged her, proud of her acumen and her ability to act with grace and style as his hostess. There were always guests at Havilah, some of them quite important. She'd learned a great deal about the running of the plantation and the mill, the diversification into tropical fruits; Harry's other share holdings in coffee, tea, cotton. Harry was not a man to invite risk in his ventures—he was a careful man by nature—sticking mostly to blue chip, but Harry would have been a wealthy man by any standards. He'd always bought her the most wonderful presents, spoiled her terribly. For her twenty-sixth birthday he'd bought her exquisite ruby and diamond drop earrings. She felt like a princess every time she wore them.

It was Jason who had all the potential to be a high flyer. Jason had often tried to talk Harry into going further afield with his diversification. Jason had been very interested in mining and mineral exploration. He had tried to persuade Harry to take a chance on a new Central Queensland gold mine but at the last minute Harry had backed off. Of course the operation had rocketed to success. To this day she couldn't help noticing its soaring share prices in the financial pages.

Megan's pregnancy had altered so many lives. She'd been forced away from Havilah to rebuild her life in Brisbane. Jason too had changed course, moving almost as far away as she had, across the Great Dividing Range that separated the vast sun scorched Outback from the lush coastal strip. She'd never understood why he had taken up the position of manager on an Outback cattle station. He didn't know all that much about cattle—the owner could count on him to learn quickly—but he did have a brilliant business brain. He'd graduated top of his class in Commerce and Business Administration. Probably like her he'd wanted to get as far away as possible—try something entirely different. Or that was all that was offering with a wife and child to support. There hadn't been any money in the Corey family. Jason had won his academic scholarships. She suspected Harry who'd always been very fond of Jason had helped out. In those days Jason had deserved to be helped to have his ambition applauded. Then came the fall.

Jason may have slept with Megan and made her pregnant but Olivia on the evidence had to accept it must have been a drunken, deplorable, one-night stand. That was what Jason had claimed. He had even confessed he couldn't for the life of him remember what had happened. Even so she could never forgive him. At least he'd done the honourable thing and married Megan. He didn't love her. The great irony was Jason had never really liked Megan claiming there was something secretive about her.

Now it seemed Jason and his family had returned home to their birthplace—who knew why—and it was Jason of all people who had found Harry dead. There seemed no way Jason Corey would remain in her past. As Olivia had learned to her cost there were no certainties in life. With Harry gone, she would have to face Jason again.

CHAPTER TWO

IT WAS scorching out in the fields. Jason, clad in a navy singlet and jeans, his skin sheened with sweat, sat in the ute draining off a soda and watching the bright red self-propelled harvesters cutting a swathe through the purple tipped ripe crop. The harvest reached an impressive four metres, stretching clear away to the indigo line of the ranges. The harvesters were lurching like dinosaurs along the rows removing the leafy tops of the cane stalks, cutting the stalks off at ground level and chopping the canes into small lengths called billets. The billets would be loaded into the wire bins that were being towed alongside by workers in tractors. Harvested cane deteriorated rapidly so it was imperative to get the crop to the mill for crushing as quickly as possible. Sixteen hours was the ultimate but on Havilah he'd seen to it no bin was in transit for more than a few hours. Computers tracked progress along the network of cane railways to the crush. The plantation and mill were run with the utmost efficiency, Harry depended on him. He wasn't about to let Harry down. Harry had given him a second chance.

He'd spent the morning organising another big planting of the so called miracle fruit, a member of the Sapotacea family which was proving very popular for both the home and export market. The fruit which came from a small compact evergreen tree had the unusual characteristic of making sour and bitter fruit taste sweet. A piece of miracle fruit made eating a lemon easy. The mature trees were covered in a profusion of small bright red, olive shaped fruits with white flesh and a shiny seed. They'd moved on from the familiar tropical fruits such as mangoes, bananas, pawpaw-papayas and lychees to jaboticabas, sabotillas, rambutans, jackfruit, star apple, sapote and sapodillas, the very distinctive star-shaped succulent carambola, and the mangosteen to name a few. They all grew rapidly and thrived in the tropics. Havilah Plantation tropical fruit was much in demand.

Harry had asked him to join him at the homestead for afternoon tea. He wasn't a tea man himself though Harry was part owner in both tea and coffee plantations on the Tableland. These days with Harry not as active as he used to be, it was part of Jason's job to oversee them. He liked to keep Harry company and Harry despite everything still enjoyed his. In his heart he had to admit being with Harry made him feel Liv somehow was still part of his life.

How he'd loved her! It still made his heart swell to think about the rapture she inspired in him, though he tried not to think about Liv often. He'd grown used to a life of quiet desperation apart from his work. He'd thrown himself into that. In the two years he'd been back with Harry the people of the district seemed to have forgotten or at least forgiven him his crime of jilting the much loved Olivia Linfield, Harry Linfield's heiress. Olivia had been and probably still was in a class of her own. She'd been the brightest, the most beautiful and the most popular girl in a district famous for beautiful and exotic women from a mixture of ethnic backgrounds. Great waves of immigrant Italian families, for instance, had opened up the North, contributing greatly to the prosperity and importance of the sugar industry. Italian blood ran through his veins, though his colouring was almost entirely his father's whose background was Irish.

Olivia Linfield was their version of a princess. She enjoyed a privileged status. A prize for any man, yet she had chosen him. A princess wooed and won by a young man born on the wrong side of the tracks.

At sixteen, his father had started his working life as a cane cutter like his father before him. Those were the days before mechanical cane harvesters replaced manual labour. His mother had been a domestic up at the Big House—not that there was any sort of shame in that. In many ways it had been considered a plum job for those who hadn't been in the fortunate position to go on to higher education. When Jason was twelve and almost a man his father had deserted his mother and him. One day he was there, a man of uncertain moods and temper, the next he was gone.

"Good riddance!" Jason's Italian grandmother had cried, shaking her fist at the heavens. His grandmother was full of drama. "All he was, was a savage!" It was true his father had sometimes struck his mother. Those were the times he was drunk—not a happy drunk but ready to explode. Not that he was a bad man. There had been plenty of good times. But his father was a complicated man who detested living his life as an underdog. Basically he didn't fit into the labourers' scene. Surely he had been clever? And handsome. Jason remembered how handsome his father had been. Mesmerizing, his mother said. Tall, muscular, graceful like a sleek jungle cat. His father had loved to read. He devoured books, always eager to learn. His grandmother, jealous of her daughter's love for the man, had called him a savage. He'd never been that.

Towards the end his father told them he had an urge to paint. Time was running out. He had much to learn. Niall Corey had always been able to draw. People. Animals. Birds. Whatever one wanted. He'd left a note for his wife saying he was following Gauguin's example. Did that mean he's sailed for Tahiti? Like Gauguin the famous painter he'd certainly abandoned his wife and family.

They'd never heard from him again.

Afterwards instead of burning them, his mother had gathered together all his sketchbooks like treasure. Jason couldn't pretend they weren't good though he hated his father for deserting them. His father had filled the sketchbooks with extraordinarily accurate and insightful sketches of all the people around him, his family, his co-workers, his bosses, the Linfields, exquisite pastels of his beautiful mother, Liv as a little girl. His father had always told him one day Liv would break his heart. How right he had been. He wished he hadn't thought of Liv now. It brought the past crashing back.

He didn't see Megan until she came alongside the car, tapping on the passenger window so he would open it.

"Hi, Megan." He lowered the window, making himself smile at her when the very sight of her filled him with shame and a kind of creeping dread. He'd never much liked Megan Duffy. She was pretty enough but an odd little thing. Liv being Liv had always been kind to her. She had even asked Megan to be one of her bridesmaids which hadn't been in his plans but it was the bride's day after all. The truth was since the night of Sean Duffy's twenty-fifth birthday party he absolutely dreaded running into Sean's sister. "Anything wrong?" he asked, thinking there couldn't possibly be. He was on his way to see Liv, the love of his life. Nothing could come between him and Liv.

"I have to speak to you, Jason." Megan was all eyes, blue shadows beneath, pallid skin. She didn't look well.

A sensation akin to fear ran through him. "Okay then. Hop in. I'm on my way to see Liv. I can drop you off on the way." He tried to sound friendly but everything about her put him in a panic. It was so claustrophobic with her sitting beside him in the car. He had the weird notion he was going to suffocate. He swallowed on a parched throat— it seemed like his saliva glands had dried up—glanced at her, paying attention to her pallor. "What is it, Megan?"

Her voice was barely audible. "I'm over," she said.

He was so frantic he laughed. "Over what?"

"Two months." Now she began to cry, red blotches appearing almost instantly on her cheeks and the tip of her nose. "I'm pregnant, Jason. I'm sick all the time." Her voice rose to near hysteria. "It's yours, Jason. Your baby. I was a virgin."

Most of the guys thought she was. "Don't do this to me! Are you sure, Megan?" he groaned, realizing with shock he had trembling hands. "It was only one time. I don't even remember it. I've never been so drunk in my life. Oh, why talk about it! Have you seen a doctor?" he asked, feeling desperately ill himself.

"In this town?" Piteously Megan wiped her mouth with the back of her hand. "Besides, I had to tell you first, Jason. You're the father. I've never been with anyone else."

"Oh, Megan!" He slammed a fist into his knee, blazing with shame. "How did we let this happen?"

"I'm sorry, Jason," Megan said feebly. "But you over-powered me. You're so big and strong. It was near enough to rape but nothing would ever make me tell anyone else that."

For all her cowered attitude suddenly that sounded like a threat. He trod on the brakes, bringing the car to a halt alongside the kerb. "No, Megan." He fixed her with a sear-ing stare. "I may have been all sorts of a fool, but I know I would never have forced you—that's not my style. You're entitled to be very upset but you must have given me some sort of encouragement?"

Very gently she touched his arm even though he visibly flinched. "You said it yourself, Jason. You were very drunk." She stared at him, tears welling into her hazel eyes and slipping down her pale cheeks. "I'm so frightened. My father will kill me when he finds out. I've never been with anyone else, Jason. Couldn't you tell? There was blood on the sheets."

He recoiled. "I saw no blood."

"You weren't looking," she pointed out mournfully. "I had to get you painkillers for your hangover. You were still sick the next day—almost out of it. Do you think I wanted this to happen, Jason? It was a terrible mistake. Olivia is my friend—she's been so kind to me. She's never looked down on us Duffys. Mum thinks Olivia's a real lady. She's always going on about it like I'm a slut, which you know more than anyone I'm not. This has been a dreadful shock for me, too. You've no idea how hard it's been trying to keep myself together, locking myself into the bathroom. Mum asked me this morning if I had something to tell her. I think she knows.''

''That you're pregnant?'' Jason moved his eyes to her flat stomach.

''Yes,'' she said, miserably. ''I know what you're thinking, Jason. You hate me.''

He rested his arms on the steering wheel, burying his face. He didn't think he would ever smile again. ''I don't hate you, Megan. It wasn't your fault. It was mine.''

''So what are we going to do?''

Jason groaned in anguish wanting to shut the whole world out. He even had the sensation the blazing sun had disappeared. Where would he be without his beloved Liv? He might as well be dead. There was a taste like metal in his mouth, but he straightened up. ''I'll take care of you, Megan,'' he promised. ''This is my child, too. My responsibility. I always knew in my heart life didn't promise me any rose-garden.''

Liv was a beautiful dream. Hadn't he always had the feeling she was much too good for him.

Megan looked like she was about to reach out to him, but Jason backed right up against the car door, wanting to smash the window out. ''Olivia loves you,'' she said, her voice so tight the words might have been stuck in her throat.

''She'll find someone else,'' Jason muttered, thinking life for him was all over. Someone who deserves her.

Gradually Jason's rage receded as pity gripped him. Megan was so small and desperate and her father, Jack Duffy was a brute of a man. A drunk and a failure, Jason could well imagine him being very tough on his daughter.

Megan needed his support and so did the baby growing inside her. That baby was his. In the final analysis the baby was the one who mattered. Abandoned by his own father, Jason felt he had no other option but to front up to his responsibilities. "Our child deserves a future, Megan," he said. "I'm not running away."

An hour later he had sufficient control of himself to face Olivia. She ran down Havilah's grand staircase to greet him, her long silky black hair flying behind her like a pennant in a breeze. So beautiful, so slender, so graceful, her smile so radiant it tore the heart out of him. He would never, until his dying day, get over Liv. Or cease missing her. "More presents have been arriving," she said excitedly, lifting her face for his kiss.

Instead he drew her into the hollow of his shoulder. He had no right to kiss her anymore. He had forfeited that. "I have to talk to you, Liv," he said, his voice conveying the raw intensity of his feelings. "Can we please go outside, take a walk."

"Of course, darling." She slipped her arm around his waist. "What's the matter?" Love for him surged inside her, then a flash of naked fear. His handsome face was a mask of pain.

The only way to tell her was head-on. "I have bad news, Liv." He led her out onto the colonnaded front terrace.

"It's not your mother?" Olivia's beautiful light grey eyes were full of concern. Antonella Corey didn't keep good health.

"It's not Mama." Jason shook his head. "She's okay." But not for long. His mother would be devastated. His grandmother would go ballistic. "It's something else. Let's walk in the garden."

"You're frightening me, Jason." She tucked her arm through his, staring at his resolute profile, the grimness of the strong jawline.

"I'm more sorry than I can possibly say." Even then he couldn't begin to calculate the full extent of the pain.

She shook his arm. "Jason, about what?" Olivia's mind was racing. When she'd last spoken to Jason, only a few hours ago, he'd been on top of the world. Now he looked utterly desolate. Even his golden tan was bleached by emotion.

Jason paused beside the archway of pillar roses, staring at the roses without even seeing them. They had been brought to perfection for the wedding. The entire length of the archway was hung with cascading clusters of gorgeous blush pink double flowers with a wonderful fragrance. "I don't know how to tell you this, Liv," he began. "It's the worst thing I've ever had to say in my life. But I can't marry you."

She stared up at him blankly. Then she shook her head slightly as if to clear it. "Jason, darling, you're not making any sense. You're marrying me tomorrow. I love you. You love me."

"I can't marry you, Liv." Grief was overflowing inside him. He raised his hand as if to stroke her cheek. Let it drop. "Months ago I did something crazy. Unforgivable."

Olivia clasped her hands together prayerfully. "Tell me," she urged, apprehension invading her black fringed luminous eyes.

"I love you, Liv," he muttered. He felt like he was dying. "I love you more than life itself. I always knew I didn't deserve you."

"You do. You do! What are you talking about?" Olivia grasped the front of his shirt, clinging on.

"Megan Duffy came to me this afternoon," he said starkly. "She told me she's pregnant."

Olivia's eyes widened. "Megan Duffy! What does she have to do with us? Megan Duffy?" Abruptly she spun about, presenting her slender back to him. "I don't think I want to know. Is God punishing me for being so happy?"

"Liv, please. You're breaking my heart. I wish, how I wish, I didn't have to tell you this, but I'm the father, Liv."

For moments Olivia stood utterly still like a statue, then fiercely she faced him, her eyes those of a woman who had been dealt a mortal blow. "I have no idea what is going on," she said in a voice so tight it droned. "What do you mean you're the father? How can that be? You love me. We're getting married, remember? Harry has spent thousands and thousands making sure everything is just perfect for us. You're lying."

Desperate to touch her, even if he could never touch her again, he grasped her hands tightly. "You can't think worse of me than I think of myself."

"Jason, Jason, stop!" she cried. "I can't bear it!" She wrenched her hands away from him, recoiling several steps. Tears welled into her eyes but she blinked them back furiously. Anger was starting to lift, to soar. She felt as if her life was shattering like shards of glass all around her. She wanted to lash out at him. Hurt him. Hadn't he wounded her to death? "Bring Megan here," she demanded, a shudder rippling through her body. "I want to look into her eyes. Lucy, our chief bridesmaid warned me I was taking a chance on Megan Duffy but stupid old trusting me felt sorry for her. She hasn't had much of a life. Her father's a bloody maniac. Have you thought of that? He could kill you. How could you make Megan Duffy pregnant? How could it possibly happen? When did it happen? That's the thing. We're never apart. Why did you never say a word? Did you take leave of your senses, Jason? Did you lose control? Why? You had me. You love me. You've told me so many times I couldn't possibly keep count. You don't like Megan Duffy. How could you possibly make love to a girl you don't even like?"

Her words pierced him like a dagger to the heart. "Booze, what else?" he said in desolation. "I must have thought she was you...but, no!" Immediately he rejected that notion.

"That wouldn't be right, she could never be you. I was drunk, Liv, I'll have to live with that all my life. As for when it happened? It was months ago, after Sean Duffy's birthday party. I told you I'd look in. The terrible part is I didn't want to go but I felt obligated to at least make an appearance. He's on my team."

She willed herself not to break into a storm of weeping. That would have to wait until later when she was alone. "On your team? To think I was so proud of the way you excelled at sports. You're a wonderful athlete but Sean Duffy...you know he's into drugs. Why get mixed up with the likes of him?" Olivia struck Jason so hard in the chest, he reeled off balance. "Someone stop me from screaming," she cried out in torment. "You had sex with Megan Duffy, my bridesmaid? That's too much." Olivia wrapped her arms around her body, holding herself upright with a tremendous effort. She had to counteract the feeling she was going to pass out. Her beautiful skin registered her agitation. It had turned white as milk. "Am I dreaming?" She stared upwards at the cloudless blue sky as though it could give her the answer. "I'm in the middle of a nightmare, aren't I? Tell me!"

Jason shook his auburn head in shame and despair. "I don't know how it happened, Liv. I can't believe it happened." His wide shoulders slumped. "I'd give anything to turn back the clock. I'll never forgive myself for causing you so much pain."

"Pain? What do you mean, pain?" she gritted. "What about the bloody humiliation?" She who rarely swore was having difficulty stopping. "Don't let's beat about the bush. You've made the greatest fool of me. I gave you my heart. My soul. My pathetic body. At least I didn't set you up for a shotgun wedding, that's what you'll have with the Duffys. And good luck to you and Megan. I'd have gone with you to the ends of the earth if you'd asked me. I was a total, total fool about you. As for that little traitor Megan, I felt I was helping her but all the while she was probably using me. You were right when you once called her secretive. I've been so happy, so brimming with joy, I couldn't see what was right under my nose.'' Olivia let out a strangled breath. ''Ah, Jason!'' Sorrow replaced anger. ''To think I loved you. Your blue eyes! I thought your beautiful blue eyes were windows to your soul. Only there's no-one home in your soul.''

He inhaled jaggedly, feeling the most profound shame. ''Not anymore.'' He'd lost her. He was demolished.

Olivia's radiance too was totally extinguished. ''I've loved you all my life,'' she said brokenly. ''To think Harry loves you. He's done so much for you. He was proud to welcome you into the family. How you've betrayed us, betrayed yourself.''

''I know.'' He felt like a man of no substance. Like his father.

''You know?'' She threw up her chin. It perfectly expressed her anger and pride. ''Is that all you can say? You know! Goddamn you, Jason.'' Her voice began to shake in her throat. Her eyes turned to a diamond dazzle of pure fury. Deliberately she brought up her left hand that bore his ring and slapped him hard as she could across his taut handsome face. It left a red stain on his tanned skin and little spurts of blood where the setting of the ring had caught him. ''I want you to leave,'' she said with the greatest contempt. ''Here's your ring though it meant precious little to you.'' She tore the solitaire diamond ring off her finger, hurling it at him, all fierce disgust. ''I never want to see you again.'' She was choking with anger and grief. ''Go away, Jason Corey. Go away and never come back.''

Jason came out of his reverie as a huge smoke-grimed hand came in the open window of the ute and touched his shoulder. It startled him. ''Bruno?''

''Are you all right, mate?'' Bruno, who had been driving

one of the tractors looked in at him with concern. "It must be boiling in the ute. I'm goin' over to the shed for a cold beer. Want one?"

Jason blinked hard, hoping his expression wasn't as stricken as he felt. The memories that had come rushing back had been more vivid than they had been in a long time. "No thanks, Bruno," he said, surprised his voice sounded so normal. "You go right ahead. We're making good progress. Mr. Linfield has asked me to join him." He glanced at his watch. "I'd better get going."

"See ya later then, boss." Bruno, a giant of a man stood away from the ute, giving Jason a quick salute as he drove away.

He had to get shot of the sense of hopelessness and futility that had overwhelmed him, Jason thought. It had come right out of the blue. Memories had a tendency to do that. With the passing of time he had convinced himself he was getting better and better at holding himself together. He was nowhere near the strong, self-sufficient figure most people thought him. All it needed was a chink opening onto the past for him to fall into a black void. Why were his memories bothering him today? He didn't even dream about Liv much anymore. He'd learned to keep a tight rein on himself, even his subconscious. He had responsibilities. Harry had come to depend on him more and more. Jason was virtually running Havilah these days.

"You're my right hand man, Jason. I'm closer to you than I am to anybody outside my dear Olivia."

Tough as nails, him. A very fast learner. Harry had never had cause to tell him anything twice anymore than the owner of Caramba Station who'd done everything in his power to get Jason to stay on. His mother's final illness—cancer—and quick death had brought him home. It had been a very, very difficult time. He'd loved his mother as he'd come to despise his absent father. But life went on. He had his little daughter, Tali to take care of. He had to make life right for her She was a wonderful little kid with his deep blue eyes. He saw little, if anything, of Megan in her. Her thick, silky black curls spoke to him of her Italian heritage though she hadn't inherited the olive skin.

He was nearing the house when he saw Harry sitting on a garden bench down by the lagoon with its flotilla of exquisite water lilies, pink, cream and the sacred blue lotus. For some reason he couldn't fully understand Jason felt disturbed by something in Harry's attitude. He brought the ute to a halt, stepping out onto the gravelled drive. Harry didn't look up so he cupped his hands around his mouth, calling Harry's name. It was too hot for Harry to walk uphill to the homestead.

This time he expected Harry to turn his head and wave acknowledgement, except Harry didn't budge. He continued to stare ahead at the glittering green sheet of water.

Jason found himself sprinting down across the thick, springy lawn. "Harry?" He'd had so many shocks in his life he was coming to expect the worst as a matter of course.

No answer from Harry's still form.

He was there, bending over to stare into Harry's face half concealed by the wide brim of his familiar white panama.

Harry! Dear Harry! Dear friend! Was loss the norm? Jason rested his hand lovingly on his mentor's thin shoulder. For want of a male role model in life Harry Linfield had become that. Harry had known all about his inconsolable grief when he lost Olivia. An open paper bag containing little morsels of bread had fallen at Harry's feet, scattering crumbs over the emerald-green grass. It gave Jason some comfort Harry's expression was so peaceful. He must have passed away feeding his beloved black swans. Jason stared out across the arum lily lined lagoon and silently said a prayer.

It was only when he had Harry back at the house with Gracie crying her heart out Jason began to think of the ramifications of Harry's death. Olivia would have to be notified immediately. Olivia was Harry's nearest and dearest, his heiress. Grace would have to do that if he could ever stop her crying. The last thing Liv would want was to hear from him. As far as Liv was concerned he was still managing an Outback cattle station. Harry had never told her of the big changes on Havilah or the fact he had hired Jason Corey to run it. Harry had never explained the reasons why. They both knew Liv would have reacted with horror, there was no question about that. So Olivia was never told.

With Havilah in Olivia's hands he would have to move on. This, when Tali had come to love the place. Jason determined he wasn't going to leave until he'd placed Harry's favourite crimson roses on his grave.

CHAPTER THREE

OLIVIA took a much earlier flight than planned. When she rang Doctor Hilary Lockwood, the head of Ormiston Girls Grammar, with her sad news, Doctor Lockwood was most sympathetic. She assured Olivia there was no need whatever for her to attend school the following day. They would miss her at the break-up party—Olivia had been closely involved in the preparation—but everyone would understand she'd be in no mood for celebrations. Doctor Lockwood expressed her sincere sympathies one more time, thanking Olivia for all her efforts on behalf of the school during the year. They had been well noted.

Olivia decided in advance once she reached her destination she would ring Grace to arrange for someone to pick her up at the terminal. Grace would know better than to enlist Jason Corey's help. The previous night she had lain awake into the small hours, grieving for her dear Harry, trying to come up with reasons why Jason Corey would have been at Havilah when Harry died.

Had he come home to be with his mother perhaps? Antonella Corey had not enjoyed good health. Some said the rapid deterioration had started after her husband had abandoned her. Had Jason's grandmother, Renata, died? Hard to believe. Renata was ageless. Larger than life. But that was foolish. There were always massive changes in life. Sometimes it was hard for Olivia to believe she'd been away for so many years.

Was it something to do with Megan's family? She had no real idea of anything that was happening in that part of the world. She had cut herself off. She rarely if ever thought of Megan Duffy. Megan had been guilty of the ageless betrayal—she had stolen another woman's man, whether premeditated or not. Olivia didn't want to think about Megan Duffy. *Not ever!* She refused to think of her as Jason's wife, much less could she bear to think of her as the mother of Jason's child. That role had belonged to her. It had been ordained.

What a wide-eyed innocent she had been. She no longer wept about it. It was the stuff of fiction. Love and betrayal. A rival's deceit. It had become clear to her over the years Megan had been in love with Jason, not that Megan was the only one. If anyone could be said to have sexual radiance it was Jason Corey. Women were powerfully attracted to him. They thought him gorgeous, his wonderful colouring, the fine modelling of his bone structure, the way he carried his splendid body. Sex appeal beat around Jason in molten waves.

But he was hers. She'd been so sure of him—she had never for one moment doubted Jason's love—she had never been beset by jealousy or the fear some other woman would take him from her. No one could do that. Jason loved her. She loved him. Neither would dream of hurting the other. Everything simply got better as their wonderful relationship strengthened and deepened. Betrayal was never to be guessed at.

Until Megan Duffy.

Olivia sat very quietly on the plane resting her head against the cold oval of the window, staring out at the billowing white clouds and the great silver wing of the aircraft. The man beside her, thirtyish, attractive with snapping dark eyes had tried to start up a conversation but gradually got the message leaving her alone with her sad thoughts. She couldn't escape them even in sleep.

Almost two hours later her plane had landed and she had collected her baggage loading it onto a trolley. Then she rang through to the house. To her surprise, no-one answered.

She gave it five minutes, rang again. Same result. Grace didn't come to the phone. She could be anywhere. It was a big house. There were a number of extensions but even then Grace might not have heard the phone ringing. She was sorry now she hadn't rung Grace from Brisbane instead of leaving it until now. That was a mistake—Grace wouldn't be expecting her for hours. She was probably making her old bedroom ready; or putting the homestead in top-top order. Many people would be attending Harry's funeral. They would all want to come back to the house.

Harry's funeral.

Olivia bit down hard on her lip. When she felt more composed she lifted her head. Outside the terminal building was the taxi rank. A taxi was pulling away. Five more were lined up. It was a long trip to Havilah. She might as well get started.

"Let me take that for you, Miss." A porter appeared beside her taking charge of her laden trolley. "Are you being met or are you taking a taxi?"

"Taxi, thank you," she smiled at him, grateful for his help.

They were driving up the avenue of towering palms. Cuban Royals. Twelve to each side like sentinels. From the moment she'd stepped onto the tarmac at the airport Olivia knew she was home. This was the tropics. North of Capricorn. Scent of flowers. Scent of salt. Scent of sea. Though the taxi was pleasantly air-conditioned she had wound down the window a little so she could feel the heat in her blood. Everywhere she looked was lush emerald green vegetation, vying with brilliant displays of colour. The great overhead curve of sky was a deep cobalt blue.

On the verge of the Wet the landscape was splendid. The golden cascara trees had broken out in bloom, as had the magnificent poincianas that adorned the grounds. Her eyes moved lovingly to the beautiful magnolias with their huge waxy flowers; the burnt orange cups of the tulip trees, the extraordinary displays of the ever present bougainvillea, the common purple, and the hybrids, gold, white, apricot, bronze, crimson, fuchsia, violet, pink. Bouganvillea was the plant for the tropics. It made an enormous impact. Towering, dazzling, drawing the butterflies as surely as the lantana.

"This is some place," the driver commented, gazing from side to side in admiration. "First time I've ever brought anyone here. It's a real experience. You're a visitor, miss?"

"This is my home."

"No kiddin'?" The driver was so surprised he almost brought the car to a stop. "I thought it belonged to Mr. Linfield?"

"I'm his niece. His great-niece." Olivia was unable to bring herself to say Harry had died. The news would travel like wildfire anyway.

"Sounds about right," the driver glanced over his shoulder at Olivia with bright, smiling eyes. "You and the house are of a piece." Classy, he thought. A high-stepping thoroughbred. Super refined.

The taxi came to rest at the base of the broad flight of white marble steps that led up to the terrace. The driver attended to her luggage, placing it on the verandah, while Olivia stood in the brilliant sunshine staring up at the house. It was large. An imposing colonial mansion painted the classic white with midnight blue shutters she remembered as always having being green. The glossy dark blue looked good she considered. It made a nice change. The colonnaded two storey central section rose proudly, flanked by substantial one storey wings. The handsome white pillars of the central section were thickly woven by the same violet-blue trumpet vine of old with its shining dark green pinnate leaves. The leaves were almost as pretty as the prolific clusters of mauve flowers.

I've never been away, she thought. The myth of her being remote from her past life was exposed. Havilah had always been an enchanted place. The wonderful sense of peace was the same. It was Harry's spirit presiding over the plantation. He had been a truly good man.

Olivia paid the driver adding a handsome tip. It had been a long trip but the driver had been pleasant and courteous, not bothering her with too much conversation. She waited a moment for the taxi to drive off, suddenly overcome by her grief.

No Harry to greet her. She was dimly aware of the heat of the sun on her bare head. She'd taken the precaution of wearing sunglasses to protect her eyes from the all pervading light. The air near the house smelled heavily of gardenias and frangipani. The extensive grounds appeared more beautiful to her than ever before, the great drifts of lawn perfectly manicured. It looked as though a team of gardeners was circling eight hours a day. Harry would have been very happy indeed at the way everything looked. She had never pressed him about business or staffing but it looked as though Harry had found himself a splendid overseer.

Go up, she told herself, move one foot after the other. This is your home. Your house now. These coming days— Harry's funeral—a possible confrontation with Jason Corey—had to be got through. Her silk blouse was sticking faintly to her back in the heat. It occurred to her as it had so often in the past, the perfumed heat of the tropics was not only sensual but sexual. Unbidden came the memory of indigo nights on the beach with Jason. The call of the sea. The way the white sand always found its way onto the rug. The grooves their bodies made. His mouth on hers. His hand on her naked breast, her body stirring beneath his every touch.

The passion that had bloomed out of them! Was it the flush of youth? She had never experienced anything remotely approaching it ever since. The murmured endearments that had welled from their mouths, then rendered wordless when desire mounted so high it stopped all ability to speak. Her blood still carried the memory deep within its cells. She would never be free of it. Passion. Doomed or not, it had been hers for a little while.

Heart burning Olivia walked up the flight of steps to the shade of the lofty terrace. No one was around. She couldn't quite understand why. There was movement in the grounds though she couldn't see through the thick screening of shade trees to the lower levels and the secret garden rooms she had once so loved. She knew Grace would have been left near helpless by Harry's death. Grace had worshipped Harry. She had been in his employ for close on thirty years and Harry had been the best employer in the world.

Olivia moved into the silent entrance hall where the white marble flooring continued. Everything reminded her of her loss especially the rich scent of the glorious crimson roses that drifted to her from the crystal bowl atop a console. Roses had been Harry's favourite flower. Despite the difficulties of keeping them pest free in the tropics Havilah's rose gardens flourished.

"Grace?" she called, remembering Grace was at retirement age and could even be a touch deaf.

She lifted her eyes to the upstairs gallery that gave off the graceful central staircase. She fully expected Grace to appear and was troubled when she didn't. The entrance hall was as beautiful as ever, the perfect setting for the works of art that adorned the high walls above the double archways that led on the right to the formal drawing room, on the left to the library. Light was streaming into both rooms through the soaring French doors. Olivia didn't bother calling again. She decided to go in search of Grace. Very likely she was in the kitchen at the rear of the house.

Olivia had started down the passageway when all of a sudden there was a light clatter of footsteps from somewhere behind her. Olivia spun around in surprise as a little girl with a mop of dark curls dressed in a white T-shirt and floral shorts, dashed through one of the archways clearly making for the front door.

"Hi there!" Olivia called, much as she would have attempted to arrest the headlong flight of a young student. "Where are you going, little girl?"

The child didn't attempt to flee any further. She turned around, standing her ground for all the world like a miniature adult. "Who are you?" she countered, staring back at Olivia with bright blue eyes.

"I'm Olivia."

"I'm Tali. I'm looking after Gracie."

"Really?" Olivia nearly laughed aloud, catching the note of pride in the child's voice. "And where is Gracie?"

"She's in the kitchen. Do you want me to go get her?"

"Why don't we both go," Olivia said, holding out her hand.

The child came towards her. "You're pretty, lady," she said in a tomboyish voice, staring up at Olivia and taking her hand.

"Thank you. You're pretty yourself."

"I like your earrings. And your watch."

"You've got good taste. What's Tali short for? I should know."

"Natalie," the little girl scoffed. "No one calls me that."

"Where's your mother?" Olivia asked, thinking she was probably one of the household staff.

The child's bright blue eyes slid away. "I dunno."

"Don't worry, we'll find her."

Tali gave an unexpected little bark of laughter. "I'm supposed to say prayers every day but I don't."

Olivia was about to ask her what she meant when Grace came charging through the swing door that led in and out of the kitchen. When she saw Olivia and Tali hand in hand she gave a great start.

"You've met then?" she whispered, sounding as badly shaken as she looked.

"Hey, Gracie, what's going on?" Olivia let go of the child's hand. She moved swiftly towards Havilah's house-keeper, drawing her into a big hug. "Come on now, don't cry," Olivia murmured, patting Grace on the back, hoping she wasn't going to start up herself.

"I can't help it." Grace's plump shoulders shuddered.

"I know."

Tali inched closer, suddenly throwing her arms around Olivia's legs and joining in on the hug. "I'm scared."

Immediately both women dropped their arms, focusing on the child. "There's no need to be scared, Tali," Olivia said in a kind, encouraging voice.

Tali shook her dark head, her eyes big and grave. "You're Miss Olivia?"

"Olivia will do."

"You've come to see us because Uncle Harry is dead?"

Beside Olivia, Grace made an agitated movement. "I should have told you last night. I'm ashamed of myself. I was trying to."

"Told me what?" Olivia sought the housekeeper's eyes. They were red-rimmed. In fact Grace's good humoured, homely face was swollen from crying.

"I didn't dare."

"On come on now," Olivia urged. "What's the problem, Grace? You're not making a scrap of sense."

"You oughta tell her," the child chided Grace. "I'm Tali Corey." Her hand stole to Olivia's arm. "Are you gonna hate me?"

Olivia stared down at the little girl in a dazed silence. What had the child just said? Her head felt swimmy like she was about to faint. "How old are you, Tali?" she asked, thinking: This is Jason's child. Who did she look like? She was neither Jason nor Megan. But she did look vaguely familiar.

"I'll be seven next birthday," Tali announced proudly.

"I'm tall for my age. I'm as tall as my friend, Danny, but I don't read silly comic books."

Olivia shifted her gaze to Grace, her eyes ice-grey with shock. "What's going on here, Grace?"

Grace began to shuffle her feet. "It wasn't my place to tell you, Livvy."

"Tell me what? That little Tali here has the run of the house? That she called Harry Uncle Harry? Where does she live? Where's her mother? What's she doing here now? She told me she was looking after you?"

"Little monkey!" Grace said fondly, shaking her head.

"Look don't get mad," Tali said, absorbing Olivia's expression. "Don't ask Gracie all those questions. Ask Dad."

"He's here?" By now Olivia felt so agitated she didn't know if she could handle the situation.

"I'll take you to him," Tali offered helpfully. "You could start over being friends."

"Never!" Olivia said with fervour, lifting her chin.

"Sure. You're grown-ups. You have to try." Tali's eyes, round and pleading were on Olivia's stricken face.

"Tali, dear," Grace tried ineffectually to stop the child's guileless comments.

"Stay here. I'll go get him." Tali's voice was oddly determined. She seemed very mature for her age.

Olivia stepped in front of her. "No, thank you, Tali."

"It's no trouble," Tali told her sweetly.

"I'm sorry, Tali, but I prefer not to see your father at the moment." *Ever again* was silent but understood.

"You know Dad doesn't hate you," Tali pleaded.

"What must you think of me, Livvy." Grace was literally wringing her hands. "I'm so ashamed. I should have warned you." The admission set off another crying spell.

"Grace, please." Olivia sought to calm her. She couldn't blame Grace for not owning up. Grace had had her instructions.

"Poor old Gracie!" Tali tried to get a comforting arm

around Grace's stoutness. "It's okay. Don't worry. Daddy will be here soon."

"Dad's here now," a vibrant male voice called from somewhere outside on the terrace. "Tali, get out here," the voice ordered crisply. "What do you mean by running away?"

"Jus' dropping in on Gracie," the child raised her voice, making no attempt to move.

"Next time you tell me."

Jason stepped out of his dusty work boots, leaving them on the terrace. "You spoil her, Grace." Head bent he came through the front door. "Every time I'm working near the house Tali makes a bee-line—"

He looked up, saw Olivia. His shock was so powerful his voice cracked on the last word. Wave after wave of heat broke over him, sizzling like he'd touched a live wire. "Liv!" The fists of his hands clenched so tightly the knuckles showed white.

Grace already on tenterhooks interpreted this as a good time to disappear. She acted quickly, getting a firm grip on Tali's hand and bearing her off to the kitchen mumbling something about a chocolate sundae.

By sheer force of will Olivia remained where she was. Her impulse was to run, to do anything but stand there and confront the man who had betrayed her. She put a hand to the banister of the staircase to steady herself. Jason couldn't hurt her anymore. She wouldn't let him. So why were tears stinging her eyes? She opened her mouth, but her throat was so constricted words wouldn't come. At the sight of him all the feelings she had for so long been suppressing sprang into full bloom.

Oh God, no! she prayed silently. There had to be something seriously wrong with her. She managed a curt nod, unaware her turbulent emotions were flashing out of her eyes. More than six years had passed yet all the old memories beat in on her; the humiliation, the anger, the never ending heart break, the physical longing for him despite his betrayal. It all came back as vividly *alive* as yesterday.

"We weren't expecting you until late this afternoon." Jason's voice cut into the suffocating silence.

Olivia swallowed hard on the rush of anger. It was crucial to retain control. "I never expected to see you, either," she said coldly. "What are you doing here, Jason?"

Finally she had to know. "I work here, Liv," he said, making an involuntary move towards her. It was so miraculous to have her standing there in front of him, looking like something out of a dream, for a moment he thought he'd do something really stupid like attempt to embrace her or worse blurt out he still wanted her. That would go over well. He had never seen a woman look so icy in his life.

"Stay there. Don't come near me," she warned him sharply, visibly recoiling.

"I'm sorry." He halted a few feet away, enveloped by self-contempt. "I didn't mean to alarm you. Liv. We have to talk."

She made herself laugh, a sound totally without humour. "I have nothing whatever to say to you, Jason. I want you to go away." There was a perverse pleasure in seeing the angles of his face tighten. He looked older, tougher, harder, handsomer. The worst part of it was that he looked like a man who was used to authority.

"I'll be glad to go, Olivia," he clipped off. "After you give me a few minutes of your time. I need to explain a few things Harry didn't get around to telling you."

"Like what?" She didn't want to look at him, neither could she look away. He wore work clothes supporting the claim he had a job on Havilah. A navy T-shirt hugged his wide shoulders and muscular chest, his jeans slung low on his lean hips, tightly fitting his long legs. It was simple gear but it fit his body to perfection. He had taken off his work shoes before coming into the house, standing well over six feet in his dusty socks. The whole effect was a stunning, entirely natural sexuality.

Olivia felt her forehead bead with heat. A rage of self-disgust was coursing through her, making her feel less of a person. Instead of responding to his so obvious manly attractions she should be remembering the great wrong he had done her. Where was her pride? She knew she wouldn't be well-prepared for this difficult encounter but she had expected more of herself.

"I knew you were at Havilah when Harry died," she said, not bothering to hide her hostility. "I know you found him. I want to see him to say goodbye."

"Of course. I can take you," Jason offered quietly. "His body is at the funeral home."

"Aronson's?" She felt the tears well into her eyes; blinked them back.

"Yes." He knew exactly how grief-stricken she felt.

"I can find it." She rejected his offer out of hand. "I don't need you, Jason. It's much too late to play at being friends. I'm tired, it was a long trip. What is it you have to say? I doubt it will interest me much. So you work here? I don't know how Harry allowed it. I can't forgive you at all."

"Can we go into the library?" he suggested. "Voices travel down the hallway."

She could tell from his concentrated frown he thought the child might hear. She relented on that account only, leading the way into the drawing room as beautiful and gracious as ever. Olivia turned to him—she had no choice—feeling a throbbing pressure in her right temple. She even tapped a finger to it. "You've only got a minute, Jason, then I want you off Havilah. How did your wife ever consent to your coming back here? I thought you were managing a station Outback?"

Jason was doing his best to repress his own turbulent feelings. As a girl Olivia had been lovely. As a woman she was blindingly beautiful. Every single feature of her face had gained definition. He wished he could tell her how beautiful she'd become but of course he couldn't. "My mother died, Olivia," he explained. "That was just over two years ago. I cam home to be with her in the final stages."

"I'm sorry." Olivia bowed her head, unhappy she couldn't offer the sympathy that deserved. "I liked your mother. I had no argument with her or she with me. And after she died, why didn't you return Outback?"

"Because Harry offered me a job," Jason shot back. "We met by accident one day. I talked, Harry listened. He always was a good listener and a very fair minded man. I've been managing Havilah and Harry's other business interests for the past two years."

That piece of news would have shattered her had she not been shattered already. "And he never said a word." The thought upset her tremendously.

"Harry didn't want to lie or pretend." Jason's eyes burned over her. She was wearing a silk shirt and matching skirt in the colour of the jacarandas. The lavender sheen seemed to be reflected in her eyes. "Harry knew what your reaction would be," he added quietly.

Olivia couldn't bear to be so close to him. She turned on her heel, walking away to an open French door staring sightlessly out onto the garden.

"I thought Harry loved me." There was deep anguish in her tone.

"You were everything in the world to him." Jason protested, putting his heart and his soul into that. He couldn't bear to see her looking so *betrayed*.

Almost violently Olivia shook her head. "He let *you* back into his life," she pointed out in a withering voice.

There was pain in Jason's eyes. "Harry forgave me, Olivia. He knew what my life was like after I lost you."

She spun about, her eyes sparkling like jewels. "Oh, that's good!" she bitterly scoffed. "You married someone else, Jason. *Remember?* You have a daughter by her. I expect other children?''

''Just Tali,'' he said, his expression turning withdrawn.

''Harry shouldn't have done it.'' Once again she tasted the gall of betrayal. In the end didn't men stick together? Harry had always had a deep affection for the fatherless Jason.

''Well he did,'' Jason confirmed flatly. ''It wasn't just kindness, though Harry was kindness itself. Harry had reached a stage in life when he badly needed help. He knew I could handle the job. I've become deeply involved in all Linfield operations, Liv. I doubt you could find someone better, or someone who has worked harder.''

''You can bet your life I'll try!'' Olivia retorted. ''You must have known one day you would have to go?'' She was unable to keep the note of triumph from her voice.

He nodded, throwing up his dark fire head. ''Sure, and I'm prepared to go, Olivia. I can't imagine anything worse than sticking around to take flack from you. I worked for *Harry*. Trying to work for *you* would make a big difference. Back then Harry needed someone he trusted to run his affairs. I always had a good business brain and we were able to turn my progressive ideas into winners. I've changed a lot of things for the better around here—Harry appreciated that. I'll always be grateful to him because he gave me a second chance. It wasn't always easy for him. He didn't enjoy not being straight with you but he was keenly aware of your feelings. The overriding factor was he'd reached a stage in life when he needed help. My help as it turned out.''

''Help that won't be needed from now on.''

''I wonder how long it's going to take you to realize *you're* not in any position to take over?'' Jason unleashed a taunt.

''You won't be around to find out.'' Olivia shook her long hair. It had grown back over the last six years. ''Where are you living?'' she demanded as though he had somehow found his way into the house.

Jason shook his head. ''Not here, if that's what you're on about. Mum left the family home to me. That's where Tali and I live.''

''And Renata?'' Her proud aloof expression softened slightly.

''She's still at her own place. She does a lot of child minding.''

''Megan too busy to look after her little daughter?'' Immediately after she said it Olivia was furious for mentioning Megan's name.

''Megan's gone, Olivia,'' he shocked her by saying.

''Gone?'' That was the last thing she expected to hear. ''Gone where?''

Jason realized he'd been holding his breath, waiting for this question to come. ''Our marriage didn't work out, Liv. I never loved Megan. I couldn't make myself love her though I tried to make our marriage work. The thing is, no-one can love to order. In the end Megan became so bitter and angry she left.''

''Just like that?'' Olivia's mouth curved in disbelief. ''Simplicity itself leaving a man who doesn't love you. But your child? How did she do it or did you refuse to let her have custody of Tali? I can see you doing that?''

''She didn't *want* Tali,'' Jason informed her bluntly. ''Tali was cargo she didn't need to carry. Megan wasn't a good mother I'm afraid. She didn't bond with Tali right from the beginning, totally lacked the maternal streak you women are supposed to have. She had some dark places in her soul, poor Megan.''

Olivia stared at him openly, too shocked to register anything but her disbelief. ''So where is she now?''

Jason shrugged. ''The last I heard she was living with some guy in the Territory.''

''Well, gee, Jason, you made a mistake.'' Olivia assumed

a laconic drawl, allowed herself to give vent to her emotions. "It's Tali I feel sorry for. She must have feelings of grief and abandonment?"

Jason's chiselled jawline tightened. "I think Tali had a pretty rough time with Megan when I wasn't around."

Olivia blinked. "Can you clarify that?" she asked sharply. The Megan she remembered had always appeared quiet and docile.

"I don't want to go into this, Olivia." Jason's tone was curt. "Megan didn't have an easy childhood. Some of it brushed off on her. I mightn't have been able to love her but I always tried to do the right thing by her. In the end I was glad she took off because I was worried eventually she might hurt Tali."

"And when did she *take off* as you put it?"

"Megan left when Tali was almost four," Jason answered, openly on edge.

"She doesn't look like you," Olivia stunned herself by saying. "She doesn't look like Megan, either, although there is something familiar about her."

"I thought she had my eyes." He shrugged.

She glanced away before she burst into tears. "Only in the sense they're *blue*. I wish I could say I'm sorry for the mess you've made of your life, Jason, but I'm not such a hypocrite."

"Once you didn't lack for compassion," he said, trapping her gaze. "It wasn't in your nature to be mean."

"I didn't say I'm proud of myself," she retorted, colour springing to her cheeks. "You got enough of that from Harry anyway, don't expect it from me. After the funeral, Jason, I don't want to see you again."

CHAPTER FOUR

As BEFITTING a man of Harry Linfield's standing, patriarch of the community, his funeral was widely attended. Olivia knew the church was going to be packed. She was right. Mourners crowded into the cool, hushed interior, greeting each other in low, saddened voices. Many more people saw, as they approached the open church door, there was no room for them in the press of congregation. They would have to stand outside in the blazing sun or quickly seek the shade of the giant magnolia that stood in the church grounds.

Everyone was given a service sheet. Olivia as Harry's nearest and dearest, sat up front with members of the extended family who had flown from all over to attend Harry's funeral. Olivia had received countless subdued smiles and nods of recognition from the moment she had stepped out of her funeral house limousine right up until she took her seat in the front pew. Most of the mourners had been invited back to the house. She saw Jason on the other side of the church, in his formal dark clothes which together with the sombre expression on his chiselled face only added to his heartbreaking handsomeness.

She looked through him. His familiarity, the intimacy they had once shared a fierce torture. They would have been married from this church.

Don't think about it. Think of Harry.

There were flowers everywhere. She had ordered reams of them despite the heat. Harry had loved flowers. There were great sprays of arum lilies, November lilies, roses, carnations, orchids and clouds of gypsophilia. Her huge bouquet of white November lilies had been placed on Harry's casket.

45

They all rose to their feet as the vicar, tall, silver haired, black and white robed, moved to a position just to the right of the coffin. He began to speak. The sort of words one always hears at funerals. Life, death, resurrection. The organ began to play. They all consulted their service sheets to join in the hymn. Perhaps there were too many flowers. They looked wonderful, softening the cruelty of death, but the perfume was clogging her nostrils making it hard for her to breathe. She began to pray for Harry; for her parents long dead. Harry had been far more than a guardian. He had been the closest person in the world to her. Outside Jason. It was impossible to leave out her traitorous lover.

"Are you all right, Livvy?" An elderly cousin bent solicitously towards her, placing a hand over Olivia's.

She made a huge effort to respond. "Yes, thank you," she whispered.

She made herself focus on her breathing. In and out. In and out. Deep and slow. Surely she wouldn't be able to read the short poem she had picked out for the service? She was amazed now she had agreed to get up and speak. She was far too upset. She would read the poem quietly over his grave. Harry had been of a generation that read poetry constantly and loved it. She loved poetry herself. Poets had a way of expressing everything that needed to be said in the shortest possible time.

Several people moved from the congregation up to the lectern to make their tributes to Harry. She could barely make sense of what they were saying until Jason Corey moved up to the front of the church. For a moment she refused to look at him but he was too compelling. For the first time she heard clearly. His vibrant voice was controlled but it rang out thrillingly in the packed church.

I can't weep she thought. She dared not start. Neither can I go on much longer. Sickness, sadness, turmoil was building up inside her. Jason spoke so movingly; once even making the congregation break into quiet laughter over something Harry had said and done. Beside her her cousin was quietly crying, holding a lace trimmed handkerchief to her mouth and nose. The congregation couldn't wrench their eyes away from Jason, the light from the stained-glass window behind the altar, touching his deep russet hair with pure gold.

How long had she ached for him? Nearly seven years. A snowball in hell had more of a chance than she had of dismissing Jason Corey. He was so much a part of her it terrified her. Maybe their lives had been linked too young.

Giddiness swept over her. She felt hot, then icy. The perfume of the flowers was overwhelming. November lilies on Harry's coffin. She had to cough. Instead she felt herself start to slump sideways....

She opened her eyes to find herself sitting on a long bench in the vestry, her back and head resting against the cool stone wall.

"What happened?"

"You passed out," Jason told her quietly.

"Oh no!" She tipped back her head, closing her eyes again. "Did you carry me in here?"

"You always were a featherweight." His half smile was brief, twisted.

"They're singing the last psalm." The sound of voices penetrated the solid mahogany door. "I meant to read a poem. I'd picked it out especially."

"Just stay quiet for a moment, Olivia," he said, his eyes on her extreme pallor.

"I'll be fine in a moment. I've fainted only once before in my life."

"I remember."

"At least then I broke my arm. I didn't intend to faint at my dear Harry's funeral."

"Of course not."

"I want to see this through." A look of anxiety crossed her face.

"I suppose you don't want me to stick alongside?" Jason suggested, knowing in advance what the answer would be.

"No." She had no choice but to hurt him. "You used to be good at coming to the rescue. Thank you for helping now, but I can carry on by myself. Where's Tali?"

He looked surprised by her question. "She's with her grandmother. She wanted to come but I thought it would be too much for her. Funerals are always achingly sad and she's too young."

That was something she already knew. She had insisted on attending her parents' funeral. But then she had been ten and Harry had allowed Jason to sit beside her, holding her hand tightly. The mental image of him as a boy was still with her.

"I don't like leaving you like this," he said. She looked very beautiful, very graceful, very vulnerable, the black of her dress only emphasizing the magnolia perfection of her skin. Years may have passed but it only seemed like yesterday he was telling her he couldn't marry her.

"But I don't want you here, Jason," she told him with intensity. "I can't make that any plainer. I want no part of you anymore."

He stared down at her in a kind of perverse delight. "Of course you don't. I'll send in one of your relatives. That nice cousin."

"No thanks. I'm okay." Determinedly Olivia rose to her feet. "Where's my hat?"

He twisted away. "Here." He passed her her very stylish black hat with its generous wide brim upturned at the edges. She was a glamorous creature his Liv. So he called "his Liv" in his thoughts?

She placed it on her head, giving him a frowning look. "Straight? There's no mirror."

"It's fine. Sure you'll be okay?"

"I have to be," she said with a bitter smile. "There's more to come."

Indeed there was.

But it wasn't until Gilbert Symonds Harry's solicitor was leaving the house did she learn the full extent of what faced her. "If it's convenient, Olivia, I'll come back tomorrow to read Harry's will," he told her gravely. "Say two o'clock. Would that suit?"

"Two o'clock will be fine, Gilbert." She gave him her hand.

"You of course are the main beneficiary as you know. But there are other bequests."

"Of course. I would expect that. Harry was a very generous man. There's family, charities, I'm sure he left something for Grace."

Gilbert Symonds glanced away for a moment. "I know this might take your breath away, Olivia, in view of what happened between you and Jason Corey, but Jason is a beneficiary. He should be at the reading."

"Jason?" That rocked her. Would the shocks never cease? Why did Jason deserve anything? He would have been well paid. Maybe it was a set of golf clubs or something, or the estate four-wheel drive he appeared to have the use of. Olivia waited for further comment from the lawyer. None was forthcoming.

"Until tomorrow then, Olivia. You'll let Jason know?"

"There's nothing else I can do."

The solicitor saw how deeply she was disturbed. He smiled sympathetically. "It's Harry's wish, my dear."

A final bend in the road and there was the Corey house. It was not the modest bungalow she remembered—this was really charming. Considerable work had been done on the house and grounds. There was a new post and rail fence painted a glossy white that contrasted beautifully with the

emerald lushness of the newly mown lawn. The house itself
had been painted an attractive sage-green that matched the
colour of the corrugated iron roof. The porch was now surrounded by a traditional timber railing painted white to
match the front door, the windows and the facia trim. White
wicker furniture on the porch completed the look of a
charming, welcoming farmhouse. The garden was bright
with flowers, lots of white and sunny yellow. An attractive
white painted timber sign on the gate said: Corey Cottage.

Havilah's estate four-wheel drive was parked on the gravelled drive.

Olivia's heart leapt into her throat. She switched off the
ignition, continuing to sit in Harry's big car wondering what
she was going to do next. Why had she come? She could
have called him on the phone.

I can't do this, she thought. Cool, calm and composed
Miss Linfield who could handle the most difficult and pre-
cocious students remained where she was. Wildly unde-
cided. Lapped in anguish.

What a fool I am! Surviving Jason had only been possible
because she had removed herself totally from the sight of
him. She still loved and detested him. She was to be pitied
really, not that she had any control of it. Her will ceased to
function when it came to Jason Corey.

Jason himself decided the situation by coming out the
front door. He was wearing a paint spattered red singlet and
navy shorts that showed his deeply tanned, long straight
legs.

For a moment she almost huddled down in the seat so he
couldn't see her. How absurd! She hadn't learned a damn
thing about herself. Maybe she never would. Maybe she
could never make a life without Jason Corey somewhere in
it. He was heading purposefully for her. There was nothing
else for it. To avoid being seen as a complete fool she had
to get out.

"Hi, Olivia," he called as he approached. "Want something?"

To her relief her voice came out with cool control. "I could have phoned but I wanted to get out of the house for a while. Gilbert Symonds is coming this afternoon—two o'clock—to read Harry's will. It appears you're a beneficiary and as such Gilbert needs you to attend." She was glad her eyes were protected by her sunglasses though her heart was beating like a drum.

He stared hard at her. Damn near arrogant. "I know nothing about being a beneficiary," he said.

"Be that as it may," she returned acidly, "you *are*. It seems Harry must have been very fond of you."

Little flames licked up in his blue eyes. "Don't provoke me, Olivia," he warned. "I served my time. I'm a free man."

"Ah well, we've both had our misfortunes," she pointed out with mock blitheness. "I'd better get going." She half turned away, acutely aware the very sight of him pushed her to the edge. His smooth tanned skin was sheened by the lightest sweat. For a sickening moment she'd wanted to lap it with her lips. No man outside Jason had ever reduced her to this state. Where's Tali?" she asked in a clipped voice.

"Is Tali the only Corey you like?" His expression was darkly amused.

"I lost all liking for you long ago. I'm *free*, Jason. Free of you."

"Fine. Want to come in?"

"Why ever would I?" She faced him head on. It was a huge mistake—taller than average Jason had always made her feel small and very feminine. His tanned chest was densely muscular, his throat and jaw line hewn by a master sculptor. His nose was perfectly straight, his mouth a sensual curving line. Dark red hair, vivid blue eyes. That was Jason Corey. A confronting, challenging man.

"Women are curious creatures," he said, his eyes conveying he was perfectly conscious of the ambivalence of her feelings towards him. "What brought you out here, Olivia? *Really?*" He locked gazes with her.

Immediately she was on her guard. "Not to see you, Jason. You have to move on."

He smiled. "Why don't you come inside? I'm repainting Tali's room," he said with mock casualness. "She's over with her grandmother by the way. The smell of paint lingers even with the windows wide-open and it gives her a stuffy nose."

"Does she have any little friends?" Olivia made an attempt to disperse the *erotic* quality of the current that flashed between them.

"Is this the schoolmarm talking?" He grinned. "Tali seems to prefer adults. She's a funny little thing, six going on sixty. Sometimes I think she's been here before. You might be kind enough to give me your opinion on the colour trim?"

"I'm sure you can come up with the smart choice yourself." She could have said how much she liked all the improvements to the house, but his betrayal would leave her smarting forever.

"Women are better." He let his eyes linger on her. She was wearing some gauzy floaty summer dress, sky-blue printed with flowers, blue sandals with a little heel on her feet. Her heavy silky black hair was pulled back in the heat with one smooth lock escaping to curve against her cheek. She looked immaculate and immensely sexy at one and the same time. "I spent ten minutes trying to decide between pink and lemon but couldn't make a choice," he told her. "Besides it's hot for you standing in the sun."

"How kind of you to worry." A mocking smile played around her lips. "More like, come into my parlour said the spider to the fly. Could you really be attempting to break down my defences, Jason?" She knew if she made one false move he would devour her. "Don't waste your time trying.'' She turned back purposefully to the car. ''We'll never be friends again.''

''Then I'll just have to live with it, won't I?'' He beat her to the car with a couple of long strides, opening out the door and waiting for her to get behind the wheel. He towered over her, much too close for peace of mind. Or body. Part of her was furious at the way they had picked up again; part of her in a panic; part of her just so busy fighting it. His particular male scent was in her nostrils. He had always been *perfect* to her. At least *physically*. It was just horrible the way she still wanted him. Horrible and humiliating. She was hating every moment of it, hating the way his blue eyes moved over her as if he knew everything there was to know about her.

Perhaps he did.

What exactly had Harry done? They sat in the library watching Gilbert Symonds, the solicitor, remove the document that was Harry's last will and testament from his briefcase. His movements couldn't have been more slow to Olivia's way of thinking; either that or her nerves were racing.

Finally he began to read from the document, face impressive, voice with the appropriate gravitas.

''This is the last will and testament of me, Harold Benedict Linfield, bachelor of Havilah Sugar Plantation in the shire of Linfield in the state of Queensland.''

What was coming? Olivia pondered, gazing intently at the lawyer and never in Jason's direction. He, too, sat in a leather armchair facing the imposing Victorian desk. Harry had never revealed even the remote possibility Jason Corey would figure in his will. And that was in the days when Jason had been hugely in favour as her fiancé. The lawyer's voice droned on through matters of great importance to her.

As she had been promised the bulk of Harry's estate went to her. There were numerous bequests in the way of valuable gifts to various members of the extended family, bequests to a range of Harry's pet charities, a handsome legacy to Grace setting her up for a comfortable retirement whenever she chose.

Last came the bombshell. Powerful enough to bring down the house. Harry! Harry! How could you do this to me? Didn't you consider the chaos you'd inflict on me? Olivia listened with a sense of utter disbelief, unaware Jason's scrutiny of her and her reactions. Jason who had betrayed her had been left an awful lot of money to play around with—half a million—but far far worse—it had her shaking her head in denial—Harry expressed his wish that Jason Corey would remain as Havilah's overseer and business executive for all Linfield operations.

Olivia couldn't believe she had heard correctly. She asked Gilbert Symonds to repeat it.

Jason turned to look at her, glints in his blue eyes. "I didn't expect this any more than you."

"No, but I bet you like it!"

Gilbert Symonds read out the relevant section again, a little alarmed by the level of emotion that erupted from Olivia and Jason. Harry Linfield had been no fool, the solicitor reflected, Jason Corey had a first-rate business brain.

At the end there was a further proviso that left Olivia fuming. What was she, a child? And Jason the clever adult? That was the way she was being made to feel. Ah Harry! Jason was to remain in place at least until such time, a time frame of eighteen months to two years was put forward—as Olivia would assume full control. Harry had Olivia's academic career in mind, she may well wish to further it.

Perhaps end up Headmistress one day, Olivia thought furiously. She would probably never marry. A committed spinster. Well, she was rich enough not to need a man. What about kids? She didn't even need a man for that. Women were the next rulers of the world, never again to be bitterly repressed. She felt strangely light headed.

"I don't believe any of this," she muttered finally, keeping tight rein on her temper. "Harry—my Harry—has sidelined me. Am I expected to be happy? I have to bow to bloody Jason Corey. I tell you what, that's amazing!"

"Not at all! Not at all!" Gilbert Symonds sought to soothe her.

She ignored him. She turned in her chair, fixing Jason with eyes that glittered like crystals. "This is your doing, Jason! You played Harry like the master manipulator you are."

He leaned back in the leather armchair. "Manipulator? That's rich! Aren't you a little grateful for the fortune Harry left you? It would stretch from here to Tasmania!"

"I'd give it all up to see you away from here," she retorted.

"That's damned unkind of you, Liv!" he drawled.

Olivia flashed a glance at the solicitor. That soul of discretion couldn't disguise his dismay. "Harry's wishes surely don't bind me?" she challenged.

Gilbert Symonds emitted a deep sigh. "No, Olivia. You can't be held by law to uphold your great-uncle's wishes."

"How's that, Liv? You can fire me on the spot," Jason suggested.

"I'm just about to do that," she exclaimed.

"I'm sure you're not," Gilbert Symonds bought into it quickly. "You're far too intelligent, Olivia. Your great-uncle is telling you something I think you should listen to. Jason here has been doing a splendid job of helping Harry run his affairs. Many the time I've had lunch with Harry when he's sung Jason's praises. Everyone in the district knows how quickly Jason has learned the ropes. It didn't come as a surprise. Jason always was an exceptional young man."

"Puh-lease," Olivia groaned. "He doesn't happen to be on my list of friends."

"It's only for a short time anyway," the solicitor pointed out, employing his most reasonable tones. "Eighteen months to two years. You'd be foolish, Olivia, to deprive yourself and Linfield Enterprises of Jason's expertise.''

A tidal wave of conflicting emotions was engulfing Olivia. ''Have you forgotten our history, Gilbert?'' she asked, more quietly. ''Jason Corey jilted me on the eve of our wedding as you and the entire district know.''

''Move on, Olivia,'' Jason advised laconically.

''I'll move you on. I promise.'' Olivia rose to her feet.

Gilbert Symonds looked up at her with a combination of sympathy and shrewd diplomacy. ''You have a choice, Olivia. Find someone else to look after Harry's many affairs, or honour his wishes. I want you to think hard about it before coming to a decision.''

''Did you hear that, Olivia? Think hard.'' Jason got up and walked to the double doors of the library. ''I promise I'll stay out of your way.''

''Damned right you will,'' she retorted with some fire. ''I'm smart enough to run this whole damned operation myself. You men!''

''Hell, we're not going to get into feminist arguments, are we?'' Jason mocked.

''I'm just as smart as you and far more common sense,'' Olivia told him scornfully. ''Much as I loved Harry, he's made a big mistake. Harry, of all people! Is there anyone of you I can trust?''

''I hope you trust me, my dear,'' Gilbert Symonds chipped in, too much the lawyer to be tempted into interfering.

''Why don't you settle down, Liv,'' Jason said. ''Harry left you the whole caboodle. All he's asking is for you to learn the ropes as I had to. You're smart, we all know that and you always did have more common sense than most, but you can't expect to operate at the level I do right off. You need a bit of time. What about your career? Have you worked out a way you're going to be able to manage the lot?''

Olivia gritted her small white teeth. ''I thought you were out of here?''

''I decided I'd make the first move before you showed me the door. I could quit right now, Liv. I'm a half a million richer. Thank you, Harry.'' He saluted some point in the ceiling. ''But Harry left me in charge and if you don't want to honour his wishes, I do.''

He strode out the library door, but Olivia charged after him. He was assuming command in her own house. The colossal hide of him! She had grown used to being shown respect. In her anger, she reached out and grasped his arm, her long nails digging in to his bare skin and she didn't care. ''It won't work, Jason,'' she threatened. ''It absolutely *can't* work.''

He wheeled to stare down at her, tall, lean, too powerful for her. His blue eyes shot sparks. ''Like what do you think is going happen, Liv?'' he demanded, his tone harshly derisive. ''*This?* Is this what you're afraid of?''

While her heart did a great somersault he hauled her into his arms, so masterfully she had to slump against him.

There was a crackling in her ears, as he brought his mouth down punishingly over hers, kissing her with a hot, hard, reckless abandon that ignited her insides. Adrenaline flooded her blood as he pushed her beyond resistance, filling her up with wanting…*wanting*. So much wanting she could never let him know.

When he let her go Olivia rocked on her feet, torn by shock and a deep running excitement that bruised her pride. ''How dare you!'' she blazed, guilt prompting action. ''What effrontery!'' The words spilled out in shuddering gasps. ''How dare you treat me as an object. You bastard!'' Before she could stop herself she lifted her hand to him as she had done once before in the past but Jason was ready for her.

''That woke you up, didn't it?'' he taunted, catching and

holding her wrist aloft. "Beautiful Olivia! The Ice Maiden. Took your breath away, did I?"

"I hated it." She jerked her hand away, passing the back of it over her mouth in an effort to wipe his kiss clean. It was too twisted to say she *loved* it.

"Oh well, I can do better." His smile was sudden. An illumination. The smile once upon a time she had watched for.

Tremblingly she pointed to the door, her attitude so dramatic it would have been funny only she was so obviously upset. "Get out of here, Jason. You've shown me what you're capable of. I not only hate you, I'm starting to hate myself."

CHAPTER FIVE

OLIVIA did nothing whatever in the next few days. She remained quietly at the homestead, trying to manage her grief and the shock decisions Harry had called on her to bear. She made no move to venture around the estate. She knew Jason was going about the business of running Havilah. Let him. She didn't interfere. She would bide her time. She was in no condition to make far reaching decisions. Not yet.

That kiss he had forced on her—she couldn't handle thinking of it any other way—had proved beyond any shadow of doubt Jason was in her system to stay. It was up to her not to become a slave to her system. She of all people knew just how dangerous Jason could be. She decided to close herself into Harry's study, catching up on estate affairs. She had a perfectly good brain. Harry had left her a fortune. It was up to her to decide the best way it could be made to work.

She fancied she heard Harry's voice in her ear. "My word, Livvy, you've got your head screwed on right!"

She should have. She'd been learning from Harry since she was ten. In large part, at least until she had left Havilah Harry had talked to her about everything, explained everything, why he made his decisions. He'd encouraged her interest in all aspects of Linfield Enterprises. She had her own trust fund, which with Harry as her mentor she'd been able to make work for her of recent years playing the stock market. She soon learned in the course of her investigations Jason had persuaded Harry to expand in directions Jason had long advised. Harry had left a big stake in Orion Mining Company for instance—that was Jason at work. Probably he'd built himself a nice little nest egg. She had to consider in all fairness, Jason's workload was excessive. Clearly Harry had come to rely on him for just about everything. The last year especially, Jason had virtually taken control. No wonder he was reluctant to relinquish power.

There were going to be a few changes around Havilah!

Her routine had developed into waking at seven, taking an early morning swim in the homestead's beautiful pool, showering, dressing, reading the newspapers, then breakfasting out on the terrace beneath the huge, white fringed umbrella chatting with Gracie as she went back and forth. Grace had received news of her legacy with immense gratitude and a flood of tears. As far as Olivia was concerned Grace was welcome to stay on Havilah forever. Grace was more than a trusted employee. Grace was her childhood minder and her friend.

The rest of the time Olivia couldn't pry herself loose from Harry's study. What Jason had said was true—she couldn't jump straight into the job. There was a great deal to learn.

By the start of the following week she judged it time to tour the estate. She decided to do it on horseback. Harry had always kept a stable of good horses for exercise and relaxation There were some wonderful rides in and around the district. She hadn't allowed herself to go rusty. She had been well taught since childhood to be a skilful rider and had kept up those skills by joining a club on the outskirts of Brisbane with its open rolling pastures.

Her zest for riding had never diminished. Loving horses she'd found was the key to success. Horses had highly developed senses like all animals, their hearing was exceptionally acute as well as their sense of smell, fear or timidity in the rider was easily perceived. Harry had often related the story of how his favourite mare, Bolero, had sensed the death of a close friend, one of a weekend riding party on Havilah. Harry had come on his friend who appeared at a distance to be enjoying a few moments lying quietly in the grass. Harry had called, but the well trained Bolero had baulked, refusing point blank Harry's instructions to go forward. Harry's friend, poor man, had suffered a fatal heart attack. Somehow the horse had smelled death. Horses were like that.

Olivia found there were fewer horses to choose from in the stable. The faithful mare, Cassandra, a gelding she didn't recognise, a bright chestnut quarter horse called Brandy and a frisky, glossy flanked bay that extended its silky muzzle to be stroked.

"Hi there, fella!" She petted the colt, making the affectionate little clicking sounds horses liked. It looked clean-bred and it had big intelligent eyes. She had her ride. Stallions and colts were harder to handle than mares, fillies and geldings, but Olivia felt confident she could handle the colt. She liked a spirited ride. All she had to do was let the colt know who was boss.

She'd brought her riding gear with her, jodhpurs, boots, a few long-sleeved cotton shirts to protect the skin of her arms although she always rolled up the cuffs. A bandana around her neck protected her nape. Grace had retrieved her white wide-brimmed panama from the box where she'd stored it. Saddled up, she was set to go.

Tropical North Queensland was glorious country. Beautiful palm fringed bays, turquoise waters, white sand, lyrical landscapes, magnificent rainforests. Nature on a grand scale. Everything grew prolifically in the rich red volcanic soil. The skies over head were a consistent cloudless cobalt until the big heat of high summer when the air turned sultry, oppressive with humidity, and the monsoon swept in from the Coral Sea. Some years, it was accompanied by a cyclone or two. How many marvellous tropical storms had she witnessed, fascinated, frightened: the great resonating *boom booms* from the heavens, the glittering crackling lightning strikes, the wild bursts of hailstones some as big as tennis balls. It all seemed to add to the excitement.

Cyclones lashed the coast, torrential rains, then it all

melted away. The flood dried up. The skies cleared miraculously. They were back to the dazzling eternal sunlight, the bush bursting into prodigious flower, miles and miles of canefields, that formed a brilliant mosaic with the fiery soils of the fields lying fallow or harvested of its cane. The thrill of the firing was in her blood; the great orange, violet shot towers of flames surging through the tall standing cane, the savage crackling, the smoke, the distinctive heavy smell of molasses in the air. The times at the mill with Harry watching the trainloads and trainloads of freshly cut cane coming in from the fields to the automated receiving stations, drawn up by endless conveyor belts to the crushers, the hum of the great retorts, the giant circular dryers processing the brown crystallised sugar. The tropical North was sugar. The whole process had been part of her life.

The harvesting at Havilah was now over. Legumes and other crops would be sown on the fallow ground to rejuvenate the soil. In the distance, on the jewelled horizon, reared the jagged line of the larkspur ranges that separated the verdant coastal strip from the vast lonely Outback. The Outback was unique. A place of infinite distances and savage grandeur. The Outback had a mystique of its own. For all the attractions of the cities nothing could match the atmosphere of the tropical North much less the continent's Red Centre.

Gorgeous lorikeets winged overhead as she rode. Last night she'd heard the bats, the flying foxes, shrieking and flapping about in the garden, feeding off the abundant fruits. Nothing could stop them, no point in trying. Magpie geese had stopped all operations of cotton growing in the Territory where the bird life was prolific. Even the air force couldn't frighten off the birds. They'd staked their claim and they won. Havilah revealed itself in all its marvellous luminous greens and burning reds, golden stubble, magnificent spreading domes of great shade trees, mango, fig, poinciana, magnolia, cascara; rampant bouganvillea that climbed up every fence and every work shed, stands of frangipani and oleander that had grown so huge they looked like trees.

It was the bluest day. So beautiful the disharmony in her heart seemed to leave her. About a half a mile on she found what she was looking for. The giant fruit bowl of exotic tropical fruits Jason had created. That alone would have commanded her respect and attention. Havilah was even more impressive than she remembered. Indeed it was obvious every last acre on Harry's huge land holding had been put to good use.

And it was all hers. Very serious money. Very serious business. The trick was to learn how to run it or put in a manager and return to her career.

She already knew what she was going to do.

Havilah was her home. She found herself most truly in the beauties of Nature. It was like finding God.

She rode down a series of russet lanes between the prettiest little trees. They bore a fruit unfamiliar to her, but rather like a small bright red passion fruit. She resisted the temptation to pick one although the trees were covered in scarlet globes reminding her it was almost Christmas. So many aromas came to her nostrils, fruits and flowers. At the end of the avenue the colt trotted to a halt. She would have to find some shade. Little rivulets of sweat were running between her breasts but her ride had been a wonderful release. It had been a liberation from grief and seemingly insurmountable problems.

Beyond the orchard loomed virgin bushland. She wasn't sure if it belonged to Harry or not. She cantered towards it surprised to see Jason emerge from the canopy of graceful native trees. He wasn't alone, he was holding his little daughter's hand. Tali was dancing along beside him her glossy dark curls crowned with a garland of delicate green creeper starred with tiny white flowers.

She tried to slam down her defences but she knew this

wasn't pure accident. The appalling truth was the weak part
of her wanted to see Jason. She only had to look at him for
him to get in under her guard.

The child called to her excitedly. "Hello, Livia. Hello!"

"Hello, Tali!" Olivia sat on the colt, waving back. She
didn't greet Jason, not even when they reached her.

He looked up at her with amused blue eyes. "I wondered
when you'd get around to an inspection?" He extended a
hand to her to dismount. "Let's get out of the heat."

Still she didn't speak, sliding to the ground unaided. Once
she had made a habit of sliding into his arms.

"I'm so happy you came to see us," Tali said in a sweet
little voice. "You're not going to tell us to leave are you,
Livia?"

Olivia didn't know how to answer. The last thing she
wanted was to uproot a small child, but what was she to
do? Cheeks flushed Olivia slanted a quick glance at Jason.
"Did your father tell you that?"

Tali's face became anxious. "No, it was Nona. She said
you'd be sure to want us to leave."

"I've made no decision, Tali," Olivia said, hearing
Jason's exasperated groan. There never had been any secrets
with Renata.

"That's a lovely horse." The child looked admiringly at
the colt who was busy tearing at some vegetation with its
big teeth. "I wish I had a horse."

"Surely your father can get you a pony? He could teach
you to ride." Jason was a fine horseman.

"And when would this be?" Jason asked laconically.
"Running the plantation is a full-time job."

"I realize that," she heard herself say.

"We're going home for some lunch," Tali piped up. "I'd
really love you to come." She smiled up at Olivia revealing
she had recently lost a tooth. A sprinkle of golden freckles
decorated her nose. There was a little smudge of dirt on her

cheekbone. With the diadem of flowers on her springy curls she couldn't have looked more engaging.

"That's very sweet of you, Tali, but I'm expected back at the house," Olivia explained gently. She didn't want to hurt the child's feelings.

"Gracie won't mind." Tali put an arm around her father, including him. "Dad can ring her on his mobile. Please come." Childlike Tali surged forward clutching Olivia's hand. "You haven't been here in ages. I think I know why. Don't you want to see where we live?"

"I know where you live, Tali," Olivia said, wondering how she was going to get out of this.

"Give the kid a break," Jason drawled, shoving a hand through his dark red hair the sun had enriched to garnet. I-dare-you was eloquent in his stance. He was wearing his work clothes, this time a khaki shirt with the sleeves rolled up to the elbow, close fitting jeans, his dark golden throat and temples glistening with perspiration. Olivia looked away. "Blackmail?" she asked.

"What's blackmail?" Tali's query betrayed unease.

"I'm just having a little joke with your father, sweetheart," Olivia said, already regretting she had used the word in front of the child.

"Weren't you and Daddy supposed to get married years ago?" Tali asked taking a good long look at Olivia who was wearing in Tali's opinion a *super* hat. "Nona told me," she said, shaking some tiny white flowers from her head. "Nona and I have lots of long conversations."

"Nona's famous for her long conversations," Jason remarked without a smile. "Some of them can damage a little girl's ears. You're asking Olivia personal questions Tali. You need to be good friends with someone before you can do that."

"That's okay. I'll wait," Tali answered cheerfully. "I don't have a lot of friends, Livia," she said. "My friend Danny comes closest. The other kids at school are just little kids, pretty dumb. But I'd like to be friends with you, Livia, Nona told me a long time ago Daddy was madly—''

"Daddy will be hoppin' mad in a moment." Jason chopped her off crisply. "This subject is best left alone, Tali. I'll be having a word with Nona."

"You know Nona, don't you, Livia?" Tali pulled on Olivia's hand. "She's amazing. She's supposed to be an old lady but she doesn't have a line on her face."

"Italians are a very handsome race," Olivia said. "Your father inherited the golden skin."

"Daddy's very handsome." Tali nodded proudly. "Danny's big sister reckons Dad takes her breath away." Tali shrieked with laughter. "I can speak Italian," she announced, breaking into a fluent, melodious stream.

Before she realized it, Olivia had turned to smile at Jason. A moment of pure radiance and accord.

He sucked in his breath as a flood of unimaginable longing rushed through him. To gain time he looked down at Tali saying a few words to her in the same tongue. Only then did he manage to speak to Olivia, his tone perfectly steady. "As you can hear Tali's bilingual. She's begging you to come with us. That's the thrust of it."

"You can ride your lovely horse, Livia," Tali decided, her face bright with happiness. "Dad and me—''

"Dad and I—" Jason corrected.

"Dad and I will take the ute. It's not far. Let's go. I'm hungry."

Whatever Jason had said regarding the lack of communication between Megan and her child Olivia thought Tali had to be missing her mother greatly. Proof seemed to be in the way Tali was interacting with her. They had only just met yet the little girl was as comfortable and relaxed around her as if she had known Olivia all her life. Of course it was well known children did take great fancies to certain people. She had experienced it with her own pupils.

"This is our house!" Tali the very picture of animation came running out to welcome Olivia when she arrived. She took Olivia's hand urging her up the short flight of steps to the shady porch with its white wicker furniture and hanging baskets of yellow alamanda. "Nona comes over once in a while," she chatted excitedly. "She has her own room and her own bed. Sometimes she puts a big sign that says Do Not Disturb on the door. She likes to take a nap. She likes to do the washing too but Daddy says she doesn't have to. Daddy did all the painting. Do you want to see?"

Olivia smiled at the child. Outwardly her manner was gentle and friendly but inside she was experiencing a near overwhelming sense of defeat. It was as though Jason and his little girl had outmanoeuvred her by getting her here.

They were inside the bungalow where Olivia noted at once Jason had knocked down a wall so the old kitchen, parlour had become one open-plan area. It was amazing what a difference it had made. The colours on the outside continued inside, yellow, white, turquoise and sage-green. It was very attractive. In fact a transformation from the house she remembered.

"So what are we going to have?" Jason asked with rueful charm, watching Tali take charge of their visitor, her small face lit up, her eyes sparkling.

"You really don't have to bother with anything for me," Olivia said. "A cup of coffee will do nicely if you've got it."

One brow shot up. "Got it! What do you mean, got it? You haven't forgotten my Italian blood, have you, Liv?"

"I promise you I haven't, Jason," she countered not altogether successful at masking the sarcasm. "It was just a throwaway line."

"Make sandwiches, Daddy," Tali suggested brightly. "Daddy always gives me sandwiches for school lunch and some fruit, Livia. I tell him I hate bananas but he says they're good for me."

"They're good with peanut paste," Olivia remarked.

Tali dimpled. "What in sandwiches?"

"Yes, sandwiches," Olivia said. "There was a famous rock star who loved peanut butter and banana sandwiches."

Tali nodded. "Okay, then, I'll have banana and peanut paste sandwiches, Dad. Livia will have—" Tali rocked back on her heels staring up at Olivia. "Chicken and avocado. You'll like that, Livia. Dad is always feeding me but my mum didn't feed me. She used to forget. She hated cooking. She's never coming home."

Olivia felt an almost physical stab of sorrow. She touched the little girl's shoulder gently. "I'm very sorry, Tali. You must miss her?"

Tali's mouth curved into a wide, wicked grin. "No way!" she exclaimed, putting a lot of feeling into the words. "She used to smack me, real hard. She called me a goddamn nuisance."

"Okay, Tali." Jason moved purposefully out of the kitchen. He gave his daughter an admonishing look. "That will do. Olivia doesn't want to know."

"I thought she did," said Tali with an air of puzzlement. "Nona has been talking and talking. She said Livia was bound to find out everything. Nona says my mother stole Daddy off you." Tali squeezed Olivia's hand sympathetically.

To Olivia it was a direct hit to the heart, but her expression remained perfectly calm.

"So much for telling you to stop, Tali," Jason said, directing a I-mean-business frown at his daughter.

"What should I say?" Tali asked reasonably.

"Weren't you going to show me the house," Olivia intervened, glancing down the corridor.

Immediately Tali adopted the role of hostess. "I'm dying to show you," she said. "Come with me. Nona says Daddy is much too young to be on his own," she confided as they moved away. "I can't believe he didn't marry you, Livia. You're so beautiful. I've never seen anyone with your colour eyes. Are they silver?"

Oh Tali! Jason agonised left alone. At the same time he had to concede it could have been worse. Tali brought him undone every time. The trouble was he couldn't stop her talking her head off. It was all Renata's fault. She spent her time filling Tali's ears with family history going way back—informing him with many pokes in the chest Tali deserved to know.

Not at six going on seven she didn't. Who knows what Tali was saying to Olivia now. He could see the tender hearted reaction of the Olivia of old when Tali told her in no uncertain terms she didn't miss her mother. The sad thing was she was telling the plain truth. Sadder yet Tali *remembered*.

Inside her bedroom Tali made a dive for the bed. "I just love what Daddy has done to my room!" she cried, brimming over with happiness.

"If I was six years old I'd want a bedroom just like this," Olivia said looking around the room. It was delightful but not overly frilly. Tali wasn't the frilly type. Jason had settled for the pale yellow trim, she noticed. She had to say it went well with the soft eggshell-blue of the walls.

"Nona made the curtains and the bedspread," Tali announced proudly. "Nona told me she learned to sew when she was four and her mama used to prop her up so she wouldn't fall asleep. Nona's been sewing all her life. Daddy said she's a real professional."

"She always was very clever with her hands." Olivia admired the curtains and the bedspread. The fabric was very attractive matching the colours of the room. There were four small botanicals prints of fruit and flowers on the wall; a bookcase filled with children's books, a soft blue and white rug on the polished floor and a large white painted blanket box presumably to hold toys at the end of the bed.

Tali, lolling on the bed, clapped her hands. "Of course!" she cried as though she had suddenly made a discovery. "You know Nona don't you? You would have known my grandma who died."

"I knew all your family, Tali," Olivia said quietly. "I'm very sorry you lost your grandmother. She had a lovely name, Antonella. She was a lovely lady."

Tali nodded, looking at Olivia with big curious blue eyes. "Are you still sad, Livia? You don't have to tell me if you don't want to."

"About what, Tali?" Olivia asked, knowing full well what the child was referring to.

"About Daddy!" Instead of speaking the words Tali decided to sing them with a perfect closing cadence. No doubt Nona again. At one time there had been no end to the operatic arias Renata had sent floating sometimes howling around the district. The more violent the tragedy, the better.

"You're smiling," Tali said. "You have a lovely smile yet sometimes you look so sad."

"I was thinking of your nona and the way she was always singing," Olivia said.

"She still does," Tali told her and grinned. "Nona said when she was young and beautiful she was almost as good as the great Renata Tebaldi, her namesake."

"I don't think Nona ever had a real chance," Olivia said.

"Neither did you," Tali decided in her own mind. "You didn't tell me…are you still sad about Daddy?"

"No, Tali," Olivia told the child firmly, shaking her head. "That was a long time ago. I'm fine."

"That's good," said Tali, springing off the bed. "I don't want you to be sad."

When they returned to the kitchen, the wonderful aroma of coffee spiked the air. Olivia realized she was looking forward to a cup. Three plates of sandwiches had been set on the circular pine table with a big bowl of citrus fruit in the middle, a tall glass of flavoured milk for Tali.

"Any more amazing disclosures?" Jason asked with a lopsided smile.

Tali winked at Olivia. "Not telling."

"Really?" Jason cocked a brow. "Yeah, well, we'll see. Eat up, girls. I have to get back to work."

Olivia looked her concern. "What happens to Tali, now it's the school holidays?"

"She comes with me sometimes." Jason met Olivia's eyes sardonically. "But mostly she goes to Nona who has a really, really bad habit of filling Tali's ears with inappropriate gossip. It's difficult when she's not at school."

"I hate school," Tali said. "The kid beside me is always whingin' and whingin' feeling sorry for herself and lookin' at my book. I'm smart, I'm inclined to be bossy, but I have a bright personality. That's what it said on my report. I'm going over to my friend Danny's place this afternoon," she told Olivia happily. "We're going to watch a video. It's one I've already seen but I want to watch it again." Tali broke off briefly to bite into her peanut paste and mashed banana sandwich coming up with a verdict. "This is just the sort of sandwich I like. I might keep one and share it with Danny."

They had scarcely finished the light snack when a red hatchback pulled up at the front gate. "That's Michelle," Tali said, running to the door. "She'll come in, so you'll be able to meet her, Livia. She likes to see Daddy. Danny is in the back. They're both coming. Michelle is really nice, so's Danny's mum. I've stayed over a few times. She kisses me good night just like she does Danny. I guess she feels sorry for me."

There was nothing else for it but to meet Michelle and Tali's little pal, Danny. Things could very quickly get out of hand with children around Olivia thought wryly. Already she felt protective of Jason's little daughter which surely created a problem. Tali's well being would affect her decision. If she let it.

Danny was a wiry little boy with a shock of brown hair and big brown eyes. His sister Michelle looked no more than sixteen, cheerleader cute, with the same brown hair and brown eyes, white teeth, big smile, voice trilling as she greeted Jason. She was wearing a very skimpy pink sundress that showed off her pert little breasts and golden tanned limbs to perfection. It would have been obvious to the visually challenged that Michelle had a serious fixation on Jason who would arouse lust in any female Olivia thought with the inevitable tinge of bitterness.

Introductions were made. Michelle looked at her as though she'd come straight from another planet. Danny gulped a hello before swerving right back out the door again. Olivia remembered the family. She vaguely remembered Michelle looking much like Danny did now.

"Danny's shy," Tali told Olivia sounding ten times her age. "Actually I don't really feel like leaving you—"

"Go off and enjoy yourself," Olivia said with smiling firmness.

"Can I see you again?" Tali looked up anxiously.

"Of course you can."

That earned Olivia a big hug.

Jason walked out with the small party to see them to the car while Michelle trotted alongside, no doubt drowning in his blue eyes.

Hot was the word for Jason Corey even with a six-year-old daughter in tow.

"Hell!" he breathed, when he returned to the living room.

"Dear oh dear! Have you discovered Michelle has a crush on you?"

He looked straight at her, his tan making his blue eyes

look even bluer than they already were. "No need to make it sound like it's my fault. She's a kid. A schoolgirl."

"I seem to remember you kissing me plenty when I was a schoolgirl. That's before you smashed up my life. I used to be wild about you."

"That's interesting. Used to be?" There was a sensual line to his mouth

"Until you got caught out."

"My experience of hell," he said bleakly.

"Hell, was it?" Olivia picked up her white panama and shoved it on her head. "Serves you right!" She walked past him, every nerve-ending in her body jangling. "Thank you for the coffee and the sandwiches. I must go."

"I have an afternoon of hard work in front of me as well," he said, following her out onto the porch. "I've worked my butt off these past two years, Olivia."

"I bet Harry paid you plenty!"

"Bit of a bitch, aren't you?" Blue flames danced in his eyes.

"I never used to be," she said strongly. "I never knew you were going to be on Havilah, Jason. Harry kept me totally in the dark. I happen to find that a betrayal."

"Do you?" His gaze swept her contemptuously. "Then think of the strain on Harry having to live a lie. He loved you so much he didn't want to upset you. You never came home. Do you know how much he longed for you to come home? He had to visit you."

"He didn't have to hire you!" she burst out furiously. "You have to take responsibility for your actions, Jason."

"I thought I was doing just that. It's not easy rearing a child without its mother. Every child needs its mother for goodness' sake!"

"If Megan was such a poor mother she needed help. Perhaps counselling."

"I don't believe all the counselling in the world would

have changed her. She wasn't cut out to be a mother, Olivia.''

''You should have realized that a bit earlier,'' she countered.

''You don't forgive easily, do you?'' he said, when the pause stretched too long. ''Okay I understand that. Have you made any decision yet? I need to know, I'll have to make plans.''

''Harry's wishes are easily challenged, Jason.'' Flags of colour were flying in her cheeks. Where he was, heat gathered. Sexual tension.

''Tell me something I don't know.'' He shrugged. ''I'm not good at conflict, Liv. I never have been. You want me out, I'll go.''

''I do want you out, Jason.'' Her words were so sharp they could have cut flesh. But then she was under the challenge of his presence. ''I don't want to see you or hear your voice. Only your absence will heal my heart.''

''You don't think I've suffered enough?''

His blue eyes were a glory. She feared to look into them, instead she breathed in the garden's perfume. It soothed her. ''I know I'm being cruel but I can't help it. It was no quarrel we had, Jason, something we could patch up. It was life shattering.''

''As though that hasn't sunk in in a thousand ways! Look at me, Olivia, before you start throwing your daggers. I hurt us all. I know that. I hurt you. I hurt Megan who's run so far away. I hurt myself perhaps most of all. You can't ignore that. Would you really throw your life away to spite me?'' he demanded. ''What are you frightened of, Olivia? That all the old feelings will rise up again? You didn't fight me when I kissed you the other day. The old flame reignited. It will never die. It's like a brand. Does it shame you that you still have feelings for me?''

Her whole body tensed as she let her old grieves and antagonisms unwind. ''You lost your right to question me,

Jason. When you fell into Megan Duffy's arms you ceased to think of me. You left me bitter and bereft. Don't ever imagine I'll allow you the opportunity to destroy me again.''

Jason's response couldn't have been more emphatic. His own overpowering emotions cut in. He could still feel the anguish of yesterday, the sense of *entrapment*. He had lived with Megan as his wife for four long unhappy years. Four years that weighted heavily on him. Four years of eternity. ''Drown in your misery, Liv,'' he said harshly. ''I no longer care. All I care about is Tali. She loves it here, I've made a home for her. She has her nona close by, and she's beginning to make friends.''

Olivia, her eyes blinded by tears, started to walk down the steps, her heart beating so quickly it was an actual pain behind her ribs. She fought for control, grateful for the sun glasses she'd shoved onto her nose. The fact she still loved him was a secret only she had to know. She turned back momentarily, her light eyes a crystal flash. ''I have a sense of commitment to all children, Jason. That was one reason I became a teacher and I'm a good one. You dishonoured me years ago. You disgraced yourself. I know you've suffered, but so have I. My feelings for you demand you go out of my life. It's not a perfect world.''

''What a bloody awful thing to say!'' He caught hold of the timber railing staring down at her. A veritable storm of emotion had come out of the thin air.

Olivia continued, her voice tight. ''My feelings for you however, don't extend to your little daughter. For her sake, you can stay, Jason Corey!''

Up on the porch Jason made a huge effort to control his temper. He wanted to take the steps at one leap, grab hold of her and shake her until her teeth rattled. He craved her so much it frightened him. ''Olivia, you're a saint,'' he called in a hard, mocking voice. ''I bet you think that decision alone will get you into heaven.''

Olivia walked quickly to where the colt was tethered in

the shade, its graceful neck bent to the grass. Her emotional stress was absolute. "Oh, shut up, Jason," she cried, lifting herself into the saddle and tugging on the reins. "Shut up and leave me alone."

"Bye, Olivia." He gave her an over-the-top derisive wave. "I'm honoured by your hate. Hate is better than nothing at all."

When she was safely clear of the house, Olivia burst into tears, allowing them to run unchecked down her face. She was no phoenix rising from the flames. Her heart was still amid the ashes.

CHAPTER SIX

THE weeks to Christmas flew by with Olivia totally immersing herself in all things Havilah. With the school holidays it was impossible to keep Tali out of the house, not that Olivia made any attempt to. She would have felt terrible had she ignored Tali's motherless plight. Besides she was growing very fond of the child. Tali was a smart, vivacious little girl, ricocheting from one subject to the other, keeping Olivia and Grace laughing, tutting or both. Tali responded to affection like a seedling to the sun. Only occasionally did she let something slip about her troubled life with her mother. That last day when Megan had taken her small daughter by the hand and told her: "I'm never coming back, Natalie. Your father doesn't love me. I don't love you. I have to look for a new life. So good luck and goodbye."

Tali at four had remembered word for word. She had no difficulty telling people her mother was never coming back. Of course Olivia heard all about Renata's judgement of Megan; "A cat would be loads better at being a mother!" In the course of Tali's visits, Olivia managed to hear all the stories. Renata, it seemed, discussed most things with her great grand-daughter as if she were a woman of the world instead of a six-year-old. Tali's relationship with her Nona, which no one wanted to break up, was a touch worrying. Renata was filling the child's head with stories no way appropriate to her years.

Olivia heard about the old scandals. Including hers. New scandals. Who was breaking up with whom. The odd murder or two. The way some tramp passing through had murdered a child of the town and left the body in a canefield. The way a friend had always told Renata her husband had died

77

but he was really in a mental institution. The seemingly ageless Renata was full of high drama to the point of alarm. She lived to talk. The only trouble was her main confidante was a six-year-old child. Still the two shared a strong bond.

She saw Jason on occasions. She had to. There were always matters concerning the plantation to be discussed. Sometimes she gave him instructions. Jason took them with an inclination of his fiery head but she didn't want to interfere with what he was doing. It was largely due to Jason, Linfield Enterprises were running so smoothly and so profitably. Nonetheless she wanted it made perfectly clear who was boss.

One brilliantly hot December morning that promised a late afternoon thunderstorm, she called Jason to the house to discuss the annual Christmas party for Havilah's employees and their families. She wanted to continue the tradition Harry had started.

She met Jason on the front terrace where she'd arranged for Gracie to serve morning coffee. The civilities had to be maintained. She disliked acting any other way, even with Jason. Besides Jason had made it perfectly plain their relationship was strictly business. Her looking after Tali more or less on a regular basis was not discussed. It had emerged as a fait accompli. Tali was the one they both cared about, the cement who held them together.

"Harry always stuck to a big outdoor barbeque," Jason said, lounging back in his chair with all the athletic grace of characteristic of him. "The kids love it and so do the parents. They don't have to worry then about their kids running about the house, may be knocking something horrendously valuable over. We get people in to cater—Marco's last year—it's much too big a job for Gracie."

"I know that," she answered, using the cool, clipped tone she so often used with him. It was a pathetic defence mechanism. "So we continue to use Marco's?" Marco's was a well-established restaurant and catering business.

"I'd give Robyn's Kitchen a go," he said, taking a sip of the steaming hot coffee. Not as good as his, but it would do. "It's in town. You don't know Robyn, Robyn Nelson, she and her little boy moved here a few years back. She's a great cook. A lot of people use her for their parties nowadays. She's cheaper than Marco but I think her food's better. Better presented, too."

"Is there a Mr. Nelson?" she surprised herself by asking. Damn!

His blue eyes rested on her speculatively. "Robyn's on her own. The marriage didn't work out, apparently."

"That's sad especially for the child. You sound as though you're friendly with Mrs. Nelson?"

He smiled. "Robyn Nelson isn't the only woman I'm friendly with, Olivia. Did you expect me to stay celibate?"

"Not really. I'd expect you to take comfort here and there, though the way you work one might have thought you'd be too tired for sex. Anyway, that's your business. I'm sorry I brought up the subject. So you can recommend Robyn's Kitchen?"

He studied her as she sat like a princess in the high-backed peacock chair. She wore white in so fine a cotton it was almost sheer a V-necked sleeveless top, matching skirt with a series of pin tucks around the hem. Her silky black hair was long and loose. Her lovely skin had taken on the faintest sheen of gold. It lit up her eyes. He'd thrown it all away when he'd lost Olivia.

"I said, can you recommend Robyn's Kitchen?" Olivia repeated, finding she couldn't sustain his gaze on her. She didn't want to know what he was thinking. She didn't want him to know what she was feeling. Her heart was no longer on ice. He had warmed it so quickly she was in terrible danger of having it stolen away again. Wasn't that cause enough for trepidation?

"Robyn, absolutely," Jason said with no lack of enthusiasm. "Give her a call. She'll be thrilled to handle it."

"I don't want her to handle everything," Olivia said, vaguely rattled by his enthusiasm and ashamed of it. "I have my own ideas, but I'm sure we can work it out between us. That's if she's happy to take suggestions. Great cooks can be temperamental."

"Not Robyn!" The firm line of his mouth softened. "She couldn't be more easy to get on with." As he spoke he half turned in his chair, staring out at the heat hazed garden. "Isn't that young Danny running around out there?"

Olivia followed his gaze. "That's Danny the Caped Crusader. I haven't actually heard him say more than two words, but he talks his head off with Tali. We invited him over. I spoke to his mother, she was happy about it."

I bet! Jason thought. In the town it was considered really something to get an invitation to Havilah for whatever reason. The Linfields had always been local royalty.

"Or I wonder if he's Dracula?" Olivia was slowly asking, looking across the expanse of lawn to where a small black cloaked, bemasked figure with the hem of his flying cloak trailing on the grass was ducking in and out of a grove of golden canes. "Tali loves all the bloodthirsty stuff."

"That's Renata's influence," Jason admitted wryly, running his thumb across his tanned cheek. "I've been closing my eyes a bit when it comes to my grandmother. She fills Tali's head with all kinds of hair raising nonsense."

"Tali seems to take it in her stride. I doubt you could stop Renata anyway."

"I wouldn't like to be the one to try." He laughed in his throat.

It was such a seductive sound! She could feel her own weakness. Where once there was sweetness, now this bitter taste in her mouth. "Something I wanted to ask you." She reverted to formal in a second. "Do the Duffys still work at the mill?"

He slewed back to face her, having checked Tali, also

becloaked in what appeared to be a white single bedsheet, was right behind Danny. "You don't want them?"

"No." Olivia frowned. "Though I don't see how I could leave them out."

"Well you don't have to bother your head," Jason told her dryly. "The Duffys moved away years ago. They bought a citrus farm much further down the coast at Silverton."

"Really?" Tali never mentioned her maternal grandparents, which didn't mean they weren't around. Olivia had scrupulously avoided questioning the child to gain information. The Duffys had always kept to themselves in their rambling bungalow on the edge of the rainforest. As children Megan and Sean had run around like little ragamuffins. "Do they never want to see Tali?" she asked. How could they not? Their grandchild.

"Hell, Olivia, you're way behind the times," Jason stated flatly. "They didn't want to see Megan, let alone Tali. Jack Duffy has to be the most unforgiving bastard I've ever met." He looked straight at her with his blue eyes.

Olivia found herself flushing. "It sounds as though you're tempted to add, outside me?"

"I'd only say that when you're safely out of earshot," Jason quipped. He picked up a small cake from the pretty bone china plate, threw back his head, and bit off a chunk with his fine white teeth.

Every damn thing he did was erotic she thought even eating a piece of cake. There were copper lights burning in his red hair. A thick wave fell forward onto his forehead. He put up a hand and thrust it away. She couldn't seem to take her eyes off him. "How strange! About the Duffys I mean," she said, barely maintaining her cool. "I would have thought they'd be thrilled to have you for a son-in-law?" Every other family in town would have been.

Jason shook his head in denial. "Jack told me the day we were married I'd never have a day's happiness with his daughter. His anger didn't seem to be so much directed at me as at Megan. It didn't make sense. Sean was the same, only nastier.'' Jason had no intention of telling her what Sean had actually said: "You should have made bloody sure the kid's yours. She's a cunning one, is Megan.''

Of course Tali was his, Jason had never doubted it for a moment. Megan was all sorts of things but she wouldn't have lied about that. That amounted to a sin. Tali was the cutest little kid in the world and she had his blue eyes. The sad truth was the Duffys didn't want Tali to be part of their family. Come to that, he didn't want Tali mixing with the Duffys—there was nothing to admire about any of them.

Olivia invited Robyn Nelson to the house that same afternoon to discuss the upcoming staff Christmas party. Robyn turned out to be very attractive woman of medium height, with a short cap of blond hair, golden brown eyes, a pert retrousse nose and a thin but noticeable scar across her cheek. She wore a black T-shirt, white linen slacks, that showed off a good figure and she carried a tan brief case. Her good looks were such that they triumphed over the facial imperfection, but the scar wasn't easy to ignore. Olivia estimated she was in her early to mid-thirties. She had an open, pleasant manner with the necessary confidence in her ability to handle a function of the size Olivia had in mind; some hundred and fifty people in all including the children.

Olivia took an instant liking to her. She wondered how Robyn had come by her scar. Was it an accident of some sort? Olivia thought plastic surgery might help. Most women would have sought advice for the problem, especially when they were as young and good-looking as Robyn.

"Come and I'll show you the entertainment area," Olivia invited, leading the other woman through the house. "It's large and it adjoins the pool-house area. I've decided against any swimming as it's too much of a worry with the children even when they're supervised. Besides, there will be so much food, and other entertainments. I'm thinking of hiring clowns to entertain the kids. Before it's time to leave Santa will arrive to hand out their presents.''

"Sounds like a lot of fun!" Robyn smiled.

"We'll work hard to make it that. Your little boy might like to come as you'll be working," she suggested with a smile. "I'm sure he'll know many of the other children and I'll see to it that he's looked after."

"I'm sure he'd love to come," Robyn Nelson responded, her lightly tanned skin going quite pink.

"I thought three large open-sided marquees. One exclusively for the drinks, another for the sweets, desserts, cakes, whatever and tables and chairs will be set up inside the other. The rest can take place in the open air."

Robyn nodded. Since she'd walked through the door all she could do was stare and stare. "What a beautiful, beautiful house this is," she commented with obvious admiration. "And so wonderfully furnished. I envy you living in a place like this, Miss Linfield. It's a tropical palace."

"Thank you," Olivia said. "It is lovely isn't it." She'd been aware of Robyn's interest. "And please do call me Olivia. I take great comfort from my home. Havilah is a healing place. The entertainment area is just out here." She led the way through the open French doors, gesturing about with her hand.

The entertainment area with the lushly landscaped garden beyond had evolved over the years into an impressive al fresco dining area. Harry Linfield had often used the rear terrace for breakfast and Olivia continued Harry's habit. At the moment sunlight streamed across the tiled terrace but there were motorized green and white striped awnings for protection in the heat. From the terrace a few steps led down to the mosaic tiled pool. The pool pavilion was adjacent. The whole effect was elegant, sophisticated but casual. It was an area to be enjoyed.

"This is a wonderful setting." Robyn looked at Olivia

with pleasure. "I can't wait to get started. I'll certainly begin the planning. You must tell me exactly what you want."

"I expect my plans are much the same as yours, Robyn." Olivia smiled. "Beef of course. Carpet bag steaks, T-bones, children like sausages and meat balls, kebabs, but I think seafood is marvellous for the barbeque as well. King prawns, tuna steaks, marinated octopus, even mullet is great cooked whole wrapped in banana leaves, maybe with a pepper salad. Barbequed garlic clams, lobster tails with jacket potatoes and roe, hot spiced barramundi…I'm remembering all the barbeques we had when I was growing up. Guests always love to help but I don't like it when good food gets burned. There's an art to the successful barbeque."

"Of course there is," Robyn, the serious chef agreed.

"And a lot of preparation. You have staff to help you, Robyn?"

"I have two full-time staff working with me these days, both experienced and excellent at their jobs. I'm sure you won't be disappointed."

"I want a Christmas theme naturally," Olivia continued. "We might check out the linen closet, tablecloths, napkins, runners. My housekeeper, Grace, will know what's there. Havilah has been entertaining for many long years. There will be stacks of Christmas decorations. Grace will want to help, she's a whiz in the kitchen but she's getting on in years. I don't want her tired out. My uncle used to hold a staff party every year. My manager, Jason Corey tells me the last couple of years it's been a barbeque."

At mention of Jason's name, Robyn flushed so deeply, it turned her scar into a jagged silver line. "It was so nice of Jason to put my name forward for the catering," she said. "I feel honoured. You've no idea how helpful Jason has been to me, he recommended my services early on, at least from the time he sampled what I can do. The community is so closely knit Marco's so popular, I had a little difficulty at first getting off the ground, but once Jason put in a good word opportunities opened up. I won't let you down," she told Olivia, her golden-brown eyes earnest.

"I'm sure you won't," Olivia assured her quickly. "I'm having a Christmas tree set up possibly at the far end of the terrace where it widens right out. There will be fairy lights in the trees in the grounds, all white, only the Christmas tree will have the traditional coloured lights. Our people work very hard, they're very loyal, this is our first year without my uncle Harry. I'm dedicating the occasion to him, so everything has to be just right."

The thunderstorm broke late afternoon when Olivia was inspecting what Harry used to call the Old Barn, an alternative site should the glorious weather turn unpredictable like today. Robyn Nelson had stayed well over an hour while they worked on their plans, making many innovative suggestions that left Olivia feeling the catering would be in good hands.

Both Danny's mother and sister Michelle found it necessary to come to collect one small person.

"They just want to have a little sticky beak," said Tali, touching Olivia's arm and dissolving into the giggles.

So alerted, Olivia forestalled the curious duo, by meeting Danny's family out on the front terrace. Afterwards, Tali tired out after her day of intensive adventuring took a nap under Grace's watchful eye while she waited for her father to pick her up. Occasionally Olivia stayed with her until Jason arrived, with Tali swinging back and forth on the comfortably upholstered porch swing. More often than not Olivia let Grace do the honours. She was determined to keep her distance from Jason.

The old ghosts returned the moment she entered the huge barn that Harry had transformed into the most marvellous ballroom and reception hall for her wedding day. She'd thought the worst of her unhappiness and humiliation had long since dulled, but it all came back at a rush. She could never retrieve the radiant creature she'd once been. She was hurt all over again just coming in here. Life seemed to be a never ending battle to keep herself together.

Don't get upset, her inner voice warned. Don't dwell on the whole shameful mess. What she should be doing was counting her blessings. After all most people had to learn to accept. Olivia drew a deep calming breath, looking around the ruggedly attractive large area.

Harry's goal had been not to alter the character of the vintage structure but to convert the voluminous space with its soaring ceiling and marvellous cross beams into something beautiful. Every post, every beam, every rafter had been cleaned and restained. A new pine floor had been laid down, polished to a deep golden honey. The windows had been left alone. Doors made from recycled timber, had been cut into the walls, each marked by strikingly carved surrounds worked by a local craftsman. Massive wrought-iron light fittings hung from the rafters. They had been custom made, the space was so huge normal light fittings would have been overwhelmed.

Olivia walked about the darkening barn making a determined effort to shift the melancholy in her breast. The promises she and Jason had made then! He had been her knight in shining armour.

Some knight.

If she had to weep, she had to do it silently inside. How strange life was! No one could control it. The trick was to cope, hang on survive. Megan Duffy, the girl she had felt so sorry for, had betrayed her yet now she was looking out for the interests of Megan Duffy's child. Tali after all was the innocent victim.

Olivia started and turned swiftly as a savage crack of thunder shook the walls. Moments later a great flash of incandescent lightning dazzled her eyes. She moved towards the centre of the barn, the safest place. No use making a run for it to the house. She had waited too long—she'd have to stay until the worst of the downpour was over. She felt quite unafraid—she'd lived through countless tropical storms. Cyclones were another matter entirely—extremely dangerous and destructive winds could reach to nearly 300 km/h at the centre of a cyclone. Even now in what would be a short electrical storm strong gusts of wind were blowing in the one door she'd left open, the double doored entry.

As she ran to shut it, rain began belting against the east wall, the one facing the not far distant Coral Sea. It was growing gloomier within the barn but she knew better than to turn on the electricity.

She was almost at the entry when a lean, powerful figure literally blew in with the force of the wind, shaking the rain from his hair and his face. His sudden appearance shocked Olivia so much a keening sound issued from her throat.

"Jason, you startled me!" she gasped. "Where did you come from?"

He was wearing a hip length hooded raincoat that he swiftly stripped off him and hung on a hook. "Out of the rain obviously. Surely you don't mean me to go out again?" he openly mocked. "It's pouring, haven't you noticed. The lightning is pretty fierce as well."

Little did he know she was one heart beat away from running out into the gale away from him. What had really caused Jason to come here now? Strong as he was, he had some difficulty battling the strong gusts to shut both doors, throwing the bolt to prevent the wind from blasting them open again. "It'll be over shortly so don't panic."

"Storms don't frighten me," she said curtly, to control the nervousness in her voice. Streams of water like liquid silver were pouring down every window and every set of glass panelled doors.

"Which, of course, wasn't what I meant."

"I'm not frightened of you, either." She looked at him quickly, looked away at the billowing storm. Now the violence of the storm was within her. It was so claustrophobic inside the huge barn Olivia drew a desperate breath into her lungs. She prayed what she was feeling wasn't showing on her face. At the same time she had the sickening feeling it was.

"Who's keeping an eye on Tali?" he asked.

"Why ask? Grace, of course. I've only been gone ten minutes or so."

"What are you doing here?"

"As if I need to tell you," she retorted.

"I'm only asking a question, that's all. How did you go with Robyn by the way?"

With every question he was moving closer. His big-cat grace struck her not for the first time his father had been the same. She stared at him with involuntary fascination.

"It went well," she said, taking comfort in the fact her voice was quite steady. "I liked her and I liked her ideas. I'm sure catering for our Christmas party is well within her capabilities. Should that turn out differently I'll have you to blame."

"That seems to be my grim fate." His handsome mouth took a downward curve.

Another blinding fork of lightning, its power awesome, lit up the dim interior like it was centre stage.

"Oh, hell!" she fretted. Look beyond him her inner voice advised. The storm would soon be over and she could flee.

"Is it so hard to be alone with me, Liv?" he asked quietly. "I can't help but see your agitation. I'm not going to push you beyond your limits."

"And what are they?" she asked, tossing up her dark head. "Just what agitations are on display, Jason? It's the storm that's making me uncomfortable."

"That's hard to believe, you've seen a heck of a lot worse than this." He shrugged, obviously not believing her. "We lived through Cyclone Amy remember?"

"All right. *All right!*" Despite herself she lost her cool.

"I don't want to be here with you, Jason, you're right about that. I can't stop the way you get under my skin, I can't eradicate my memories, either, though. I've tried."

"You think my memories don't weigh me down?" he countered, moving ever closer to her. The sleekness and strength, the magnificent insouciance.

"What are you doing here in this place?" He looked around, his blue eyes moody in his striking face. "I hate coming in here."

"I'm not surprised," she said with bitter humour. "Harry spent a fortune doing it up for us."

"Harry was the most generous man in the world."

"He loved you well enough didn't he? Half a million— I don't care about that—I've come to see you made many times that for Harry—probably for yourself as well—because you're smart, Jason. We all knew that."

He stared into her face, his expression suggesting his own temper was rising. "Are you trying to say I manipulated myself into Harry's affections along with his affairs? Harry was my friend, Olivia. I know he was bitterly disappointed and shocked at what I did, but I've done my time."

"What, four years?" She raised delicate black brows. "That was a pretty light sentence."

"Not if you knew Megan," he said, the line of his mouth distorted by the grimness of his memories. "Megan had real problems."

"I imagine most women would have a real problem living with a man who didn't love them," Olivia said.

"All the more reason for her to love her child," Jason spoke curtly. "If Megan hadn't left of her own accord I would have been driven to throw her out. It was getting so I was desperately worried about leaving Tali with her. Megan found it only too easy to take her frustrations out on a small child. Jack Duffy was a violent man. I guess Megan and Sean, let alone that poor worn woman he married, were on the receiving end of Duffy's black moods. That sort of behaviour, unfortunately, can get passed on.''

Olivia dipped her head, swallowing on the hard knot in her throat. ''Why did I ever ask her to be one of my brides-maids,'' she questioned with deep regret. ''Not that that would have changed anything. Of course she was in love with you, Jason.'' She looked up to meet his eyes. ''Some part of me knew that, but then all the girls were in love with you. I didn't pay sufficient attention. You were mine. My love had transformed you into something you weren't.''

''To hell with that!'' he said explosively. ''I'm tired of your heavy judgements, Liv. People make mistakes. You're not the sweetly tender girl I remember, you've grown cruel and sharp. Maybe you can tell me how the hell Megan de-veloped such a crush on me?'' he asked in extreme irrita-tion. ''I can't remember a damned thing I ever did that would have given her the slightest encouragement.''

''Why didn't you ask her, not me?'' His insults had stung her.

''She told me she couldn't remember when she wasn't in love with me,'' he admitted in the bleakest tones. ''Megan Duffy! She fooled us all.''

''She certainly fooled me,'' Olivia replied, lifting her voice above the raging storm. ''You do have Tali, how-ever...you have a daughter, a very special little girl. She could have been mine. I'll be twenty-seven next birthday, I thought I'd have probably two children by now. I've lost years, Jason, because of you. I wanted to have my children when I was young.''

He let his eyes move over every feature of her face. So beautiful! Eyes the colour of silver, mouth the colour of crushed strawberries. Only sheer force of will prevented him from pulling her into his arms. ''You're not going to tell me twenty-seven is too old?'' he asked, his expression chal-lenging.

''I can't have a child by a man I don't love, Jason,'' she

said simply. "I don't love anyone. Love has seeped right out of me."

His half smile was tight. "I can't believe you haven't had other men in your life, Liv. You're a beautiful, passionate woman."

"I was a passionate woman," she corrected, shaking her head. "Let me ask you. Are you and Megan divorced?"

"Of course we're divorced," he clipped off. "Megan took off with some guy that worked on the station. She's probably moved in with someone else in the meantime. Megan wasn't the quiet, submissive little person she appeared to be, that was a front. The real Megan you could write into a soap opera."

Olivia had no lingering doubts about that. "How do you know she won't come back into your life at some point demanding Tali back?'

"Olivia, Megan dumped her child like—"

"You dumped me?" It shot out before she knew it.

"You couldn't resist that, could you? The facts are I didn't dump you for a girl I was mad about. I got blind drunk and made Megan Duffy of all people pregnant. I just have to consider, too, brother Sean or one of his stupid friends could have spiked my drink. They'd see that as a huge joke. Let's take Corey down a peg. Megan won't come back—she told me plainly enough she didn't want to be saddled with a child, any child."

"Then she should have avoided pregnancy," Olivia said, the words catching in her throat. "There's something inherently wrong about a mother not loving her child."

"Plenty don't," Jason said and shook his head. "Mothers harming their children is not that uncommon, sad to say. The trouble with you is you haven't lived in the real world, Olivia. You're still the princess in the ivory tower."

"Well this princess isn't living happily ever after," Olivia pointed out, the expression on her face betraying her intensity. "Oh!" She jumped in reaction, as another great thunderhead exploded like a bomb. ''I want to get out of here.''

''Settle down.'' He stared at her as she backed away.

''Excuse me? You're not looking all that calm.''

A searing white light more blinding than brilliant sunshine irradiated the barn again. Olivia, her nerves stretched taut, made a dash for the door. She didn't care if she got soaked, struck by lightning, whatever. Panic had taken hold. She couldn't withstand Jason and she knew it. There was a price to be paid for this kind of obsession.

''Don't be a fool! Liv, come back.'' He caught her up and without thinking spun her into his arms. Such multilayered disturbances were within him, such lavish arousal it was impossible for him not to lower his head, covering her mouth with his, stifling her shocked exhalation.

''Why do I want you,'' he muttered, moving his mouth back and forth over her exquisitely supple lips. ''You, always you.'' He forced her head back into the crook of his shoulder so he could kiss her long curving throat. ''Judge and executioner!''

Tears stung her eyes. Was that what she was to him? Everywhere he touched her scorched. His hand on her breast was molten, her nipples rising into full bud, excruciatingly sensitive. Pain accompanying pleasure. She was trembling in his powerful embrace, aware of the hard brush of his arousal against her. His fingers were sliding through her long hair as they used to, knotting a handful to gain hold of her head so he could kiss her more deeply. He was pulling her up to him, into him, effortlessly. She wasn't even sure if her feet touched he polished floor. She could feel her own high voltage response, the involuntary clutches and clawings deep in her womb.

Was it passion or a kind of male-female warfare? He only had to touch her and she caved in. This man who had walked out then back into her life. It wasn't to be borne.

He wanted her to submit completely, that's what he

wanted. The primacy of the dominant male wasn't just talk. He thought he owned her. She arched herself back against his steely arms, but it only brought her pelvis and her throbbing mound into more intimate contact with his sex. The bloodrush to her core! For long moments she was lost in a perverse wildness, grinding her body against his, her flesh mocking her will, her rhythms fully attuned to his.

She felt white-hot with desire, dismayed and transported by her own abandon. She had the feeling he wouldn't stop until he had complete domination. Wasn't that what she really wanted? He made it all so easy.

Seduction.

And she wasn't the only woman to enjoy it.

The thought cleared her brain as quickly as if someone had run at her with a vial of smelling salts. Jason had to suffer for what he had done to her. The wasted years! They could never have them back. He made love so marvellously she'd been lulled even momentarily into thinking he still loved her.

What blindness! What carelessness with her body. She understood how passion strung even the most cautious along ruining lives. Jason hadn't been celibate all these years. He'd had women in his bed, naked in the darkness, loving them, teasing their nipples with his teeth; whispering endearments as he plunged deep into them until they near fainted with rapture. Probably Robyn Nelson was one of his conquests. Nice Robyn who blushed at the very mention of his name. Who could blame her!

"Damn you, Jason! Stop it! Be done!" Shocked by her own action Olivia twisted her dark head and nipped at his golden throat with her teeth, in the next instant feeling sick. She had no idea she could bring herself to do such a primitive thing. That wasn't a playful nip. It was like a tigress warning its mate.

He gave the tiniest little yelp. It sounded more amused

than angry. "Darling, Liv," he drawled, "you never cease
to amaze me. What are you trying to do, raise blood?"

"I shouldn't have done that. It was horrible." It was the
closest she was going to get to an apology.

"So don't do that again. It's actually more of a turn-on
than anything else."

His arms were twined around her waist, his male strength
formidable. "Let go, Jason," she gritted, her face opalescent
in the gloom.

He pulled her closer. They might have been fused together. "My Liv! The girl I loved and lost."

"This is insanity."

"More like Heaven!" He half laughed. "What's insane
about a man and a woman wanting each other? You're absolutely wonderful to make love to. I suppose if I'd married
you, you'd have sent me to an early grave. There is such a
thing as too much wild sex."

"Not in *my* life," she flared, waiting for the trembling in
her body to subside. Rain was still pelting at the windows
and doors though the volume of sound on the roof had less-
ened. With a great effort she wrenched herself away from
him, stepping back, gasping, swaying a bit, angered when
she saw his expression soften. She didn't want any tenderness from him, now or ever! "Did you see me come in
here?" she demanded. "Tell the truth."

"Say what?" He feigned perplexity.

"Tell me the truth." She looked him straight in his burning blue eyes.

"No, Liv." Those eyes were mocking. "I don't like making a fool of myself any more than you do. But hell, when
we're alone what else can we do? So you're ashamed you
still react the same way? I can't seem to find a solution any
more than you can. I want you—what's more I'm going to
have you—we both know that. It's our weakness, Liv, I
guess we have to live with it. Now before I drag you back
into my arms like the caveman you turn me into, I'm going

to find my way up to the house to pick up my Tali. You can stay here and watch me go.''

''Goodbye then!'' She flashed him a glance out of her large, luminous eyes. How could she be so angry, yet teetering on the brink of tears? ''How many other women do you actually tell all that stuff to?'' she asked scornfully.

''Only you, princess.'' He shouldered into his raincoat, saluted her. Then he was gone into the pouring rain.

CHAPTER SEVEN

FOR the Christmas party Olivia wore a dress of red silk. She didn't wear a lot of red, though when she did people always told her how much it suited her, but it was Christmas and scarlet was one of the traditional Christmas colours.

The camisole bodice of the short party dress was held by spaghetti straps, the skirt lavishly decorated with scarlet beads and small blue daisies sequinned with yellow at the centre. Her dark hair was down, brushed over her shoulders and held back by a pair of very fancy combs studded with multicoloured crystals. Her legs were bare in the heat. She wore strappy high heeled sandals the same colour as her dress. She knew she'd be a little more dressed up than her guests, but then she was the hostess and she had nothing else with her in festive colours.

She always took care with what she wore, adhering to the classic elegance of silk blouses and slim skirts for school with a matching jacket for the cooler weather. It was nice to wear something striking for a change. She remembered with sadness and affection Harry had always liked her in red. He said the colour showed off her skin and her eyes. Once it had been such a delight, such an excitement to dress, to make herself beautiful for Jason. His blue eyes on her, the expression in them bringing a flush to her cheeks, raising the beat of her heart. Jason, of course, would be at the party tonight.

Olivia pulled the drapes aside and stood at an upstairs window looking out over the rear garden. Very shortly the first of the guests would be arriving. The grounds looked marvellous, a radiance of white fairy lights strung out on the trees. The Christmas tree on the terrace soared twenty feet to the purplish-black velvet sky. Tonight the sky was dominated not by the stars, but by the full copper moon of the tropics over which it sailed. The lightest breeze was blowing, suspending the sweet fragrance of all summer's flowers in the warm air. The marquees, two to either side, one set back in the middle were white with a green trim on the scalloped sides. The marquee in the middle was set with circular tables and chairs, the chairs decorated with big tartan bows in red, green and gold, the tables alternating red and green tablecloths and napkins. Everything looked wonderful, she felt good about it.

"This is for you, Harry," she said softly. Everything she knew about her uncle told her in placing Jason on Havilah Harry thought he had been doing the right thing. Perhaps he'd believed—he was such a romantic at heart—he'd be offering her and Jason the opportunity to come together again.

A love-conquers-all type of strategy. Harry the eternal optimist.

By nine o'clock the party was in full swing. Olivia spent so much time attending her guests she had little time to eat. Not that she was a great one to eat at parties. She didn't know why, perhaps it was the constant buzz of excitement. With responsibility but not her authority taken off Grace she was enjoying herself immensely, looking after people but just as often sitting down at a table to have a good talk. She knew all these families as they knew her.

The food was perfect and there was plenty of it as always. Just as Olivia expected, the children, dressed in bright clothes and party hats, swooped on the sausages, the kebabs and the meatballs, piling the rest of their plates not with any one of a dozen different salads but the pasta dishes. Tomato sauce was a big favourite. Tali, small and very pretty even with her missing tooth, cheeks pink with excitement, her thick glossy hair falling in a cascade of ringlets Renata had fashioned around her finger had taken over the unofficial job of looking after the younger children assisted by her shadow, Danny. Danny had been invited—Tali had been shocked at the very idea he wouldn't be—though none of Danny's family actually worked for Linfield Enterprises. Exceptions had to be made for Tali's special friend.

The endearingly eccentric Renata, black eyes gleaming, high colour from a liberal application of blusher on her scarcely lined cheeks, brilliant splash of scarlet on her lips, smelling inexplicably of tutti-fruitti ice cream, arrived early, amazingly chic in a brilliantly patterned patio dress she had designed and made herself. Equally amazing were the pendant earrings that fell from her sagging earlobes. They had been fashioned by herself from diamonds, rubies and emeralds she found at the craft shop. Olivia spoke to her for several minutes on arrival, receiving hugs, kisses, the warmest of greetings in rapid fire mellifluous Italian. Olivia often thought it was the most beautiful language in the world.

"So much we owe to the Linfields!" Renata, hands gesticulating, exclaimed dramatically for all to hear. "You look so beautiful, Olivia. More beautiful than ever. That dress is magic. So sexy! I might have designed it myself. It is going to be a wonderful New Year for you, *cara.*" Renata gave her secret smile and leaned closer. "I am psychic as you know. The pain will disappear. You will be happy as you used to be. Understand me?"

Olivia didn't answer. Renata didn't expect her to answer but they both knew what she meant.

The words were delivered from close behind her; the voice hauntingly familiar. "So far, I'm pretty certain, you haven't had a bite to eat?"

She had done well keeping her distance from Jason—a protective measure—now she had to turn to face him. "Oddly enough I'm not all that hungry."

"The food is superb." His eyes moved from the terrace to the tables and chairs that had been set up in the grounds. Everyone appeared to be enjoying themselves immensely. Some of the children had started to run wild and had to be checked by a family member.

Olivia nodded. "I can see that, I've heard all the compliments. Robyn deserves a bonus. I'll see that she gets it. She's worked very hard...so have her helpers."

Jason's mouth curved in a smile. "She's thrilled to be doing it, Liv. It's quite a feather in her cap. Robyn's had it tough but she's a gutsy lady. And she's set Gracie free to enjoy herself. I'd rate this evening as a great success. Why don't you let me get you something right now?" he suggested. "You can't be thinking of your figure?" He made it sound like a little taunt, but it was really his opportunity to let his eyes roam over her. He'd looked his fill from a distance, now she was near enough to draw into his arms.

Not a good idea. Knowing her so well he realized Olivia was making full use of her protective strategies. She hadn't come near him beyond greeting him on arrival. He hadn't pushed himself forward, either. He'd waited until now when the main course was almost over and people were moving towards the marquee where long linen covered trestles were laden with the most delicious desserts.

He loved her dress, a confection of silk. The bright flush of colour was a marvellous foil for her dark hair, her silver-grey eyes and magnolia skin. He loved the way she had arranged her hair tonight. It showed off her pretty, close set ears and the line of her throat. He revelled in Olivia's beauty. He always had. "So what's it to be?" He stood before her, so much taller. She was taller than average for a woman yet she had always seemed small to him. "Seafood, maybe lobster, a little salad? Robyn's been very innovative with the salads, all the fresh vegetables she uses are organic. One of our farms supplies them, as they do the house."

"Yes, I know." Olivia looked into his sapphire eyes. She could see him very clearly in the bright illumination from the trees, with their countless sparkling clusters and diamond necklaces of globes; the blaze of his faintly wind-blown hair, the polished tan of his skin. He didn't wear a jacket in the tropical heat but his deep blue shirt was of the finest cotton, the cuffs of the long sleeves, casually turned back, his slacks the colour of sand. The leather belt bore a discreet designer logo. He looked good enough to model. He had the Italian pedigree and it showed in his effortless style. "I don't think I can eat right now, Jason. I do pay attention to what I eat, but I don't diet. It's just that I'm not hungry, I suppose it's a slight case of nerves. I did want this evening to be a success."

"Then you can relax. Obviously everyone's having a whale of a time. They will be staggering home with so much wonderful food. You have to have coffee and dessert at least. The grand finale. What about a glass of wine?" He lifted a hand to signal one of the young waiters who was circling the grounds.

"Champagne." Jason took two glasses from the silver tray, passing one to Olivia. "Thank you." He nodded to the waiter, who smiled and moved on. "There's an empty table. Let's sit down."

They moved back a few feet, Olivia sipping at the cold champagne. The best value French without going over the top, fresh and delicate yet with quite vigorous bubbles. It was lovely. "What did you mean about Robyn's having a tough time?" she asked, when they were seated. "Were you referring to her marriage?"

He paused a moment. "I'm sure she'll get around to telling you. You made quite an impression."

"I see." Olivia stared at him over the top of her glass. "You're not going to tell me."

"Obviously some things were told to me in confidence."

"Okay I respect that, but you did bring up the subject

yourself. You said let's see—she'd had it tough and she was a gutsy lady—one would have to wonder about the scar on her cheek? I hope it had absolutely nothing to do with ill treatment. She told me she was divorced. Her little boy Steven, is here tonight.''

"Tali's taking care of him.'' Jason nodded. ''She's got more of a maternal streak at six than her mother ever had.''

"She's a wonderful little girl,'' Olivia said, a tender smile on her lips. ''She doesn't look like Megan, or any of the Duffys for that matter.''

"Well as I keep saying, you can't miss my blue eyes.''

"Different setting,'' Olivia answered absently, having decided that from day one. ''Is Robyn one of your women?''

His expression was veiled. ''What right do you have to ask that, Olivia?''

"No right at all,'' she apologised. ''Except you're a dangerous man, Jason. If Robyn has had an unhappy, violent past, I wouldn't want you to hurt her.''

There was a flicker of anger in his blue eyes. ''When are you going to understand I don't go around deliberately hurting women.''

"Ignorance of what you're doing is no defence.''

"I didn't set out to cheat on you, Olivia. I was drunk or drugged, what's the difference? You passed your judgement—it was a first-degree crime.''

Olivia looked away, knowing she would never be immune to the intense sexual assault he had on her senses. ''Don't let's talk about it,'' she said, composing herself as best she could. ''Not tonight. It's all in the past. I just thought I'd point out you can't go around grabbing me with your very strong hands, then expect me to shut up while you continue on your winning ways. I like Robyn.''

"I'm glad. She likes you. Shouldn't you be minding your own business? To put you straight Robyn and I are friends. Just that.''

"Brilliant! It was kind of you to offer her support, I mean

that, I just want to be sure you haven't got it in your mind the two of us might patch up the old scars and start again? I'm not such a fool I don't know I'm quite a catch these days, Harry made sure of that.''

He shot her a look that had excitement fanning right to her extremities. ''You'd be quite a catch if you were penniless, though you'll never be the sweet girl you once were. You've become rather acid tongued, my dear Olivia.''

''I'm not your dear Olivia, Jason.'' She cut him short.

''Are you sure about that? I guess it all has its roots in our shared past. I don't mean that we were on the verge of getting married which I destroyed with my utter worthlessness. I mean our childhood, our adolescence. The bonding was very strong.''

''All the more reason I was devastated when you let me down. But I thought we'd agreed to forget it.''

''You're the one who can't swallow your pride,'' he retorted. ''Blessed are the merciful, Olivia. For mercy they shall find.''

''I had to find out the hard way. You're still here aren't you, Jason?'' she challenged. ''Tali is running around happily. There she goes, with a dozen kids in tow. I look on that as being merciful.''

''Sure, maybe even smart,'' he said suggestively. ''You can't run Harry's kingdom yet, Olivia.''

''I'm working on it.''

He gave her a charged smile. ''There's going to be dancing. Game to dance with me?''

''Frankly, no. I'm just fine where I am. You're a truly sexy man, Jason and that would be too nerve-wracking.''

''People used to stop to watch us years ago.'' He reminded her.

''I think it was more the women stopped to watch you. You could have given lessons.''

He laughed in recollection. ''Actually I got all my lessons off Renata. Isn't she a sight tonight?''

Olivia couldn't not smile. "She's an amazing woman."

"If she'd just cut a bit of the drama. I don't want her sharing too many family secrets with Tali. A lot of them are pure invention. My grandmother is by way of being a fantasist. Would you like me to get you coffee and cake? It won't take long." He tossed off the rest of his champagne and rose to his feet.

She knew she should make some excuse but somehow that was impossible. Lights blazed from every room of the house, raying across the grounds. They were cocooned beneath the trees, the copper moon sailed down the sky, smell of flowers, smell of delectable food, gaily dressed little children flashing around the garden to shrieks of laughter, guests making the effort to stare across at them sitting together—everyone knew their story—Jason's beautiful blue eyes gazing down on her. Christmas parties had their own enchantment.

"That'll be lovely!" she breathed.

It was only after he walked away across the grass to the marquee she thought, please, please, let me be doing the right thing. Jason had shattered her world once. He could very easily do it again.

The manager of the mill, Salvatore De Luca, a long time Linfield employee played Santa Claus to perfection—and with little padding. Salvatore as a young man had been a mere stripling. In his late fifties he had grown as round as a barrel which was great for the costume at least. He had a big hearty laugh and natural good humour as well.

Olivia had gone to a lot of trouble choosing the gifts for the children from a catalogue supplied by a large toy shop and delivered to the house, beautifully wrapped. There was nothing cheap; they were well made toys to last. They were received with lots of cheers and happy smiles. Olivia realized she'd had no need to fear this party wouldn't be as successful as in Harry's day. Guests as they were leaving with their overexcited children made it very clear they had had a marvellous time.

Mrs. De Luca held onto Olivia's arms telling her how much they had all enjoyed themselves, Salvatore, her husband, his still attractive, sun-weathered face beaming with pride introduced the young couple who had arrived to drive them home.

"Ah, here's my Carlo!" He slung an arm around the shoulder of the handsome young man who was now smiling at Olivia, holding out his hand.

"Carlo, how lovely to see you," Olivia exclaimed in genuine delight, staring into Carlo De Luca's bright blue eyes. "It's years, isn't it? You look great. You must be through Medicine?"

"Doctor. He's a doctor!" Both parents cried in unison, obviously very proud of their son. They had worked hard to give their two children—boy and girl—a good education. "Doctor De Luca now. We must all be very respectful," Salvatore joked. "And this is our lovely Leanne—soon to be family—Leanne Grant."

"My fiancée." Carlo put a proprietorial arm around the waist of a pretty, well built young woman with gold flecked green eyes, a wide smile and long straight brown hair, drawing her further into the circle. "Leanne meet Olivia, our local princess."

"I don't believe everyone keeps calling me that," Olivia gave the other young woman a wry smile, taking Leanne's extended hand. "Why didn't you two come along tonight?" she asked. "That would have been lovely."

"You had your numbers to cater to." Carlo gave an attractive shrug. "We didn't like to intrude."

"You wouldn't have been intruding at all. How long are you here for?"

"Day after Boxing Day," Carlo said, leaning sideways to kiss his fiancée's temple. "I'll be back on duty at the hospital day after that. Leanne is a physiotherapist, she'll be back at work, too."

"I'd love it if you could fit in a visit before you go," Olivia said. "Perhaps dinner? I can invite a few friends over. People you know, Carlo, I'm sure they'd love to meet Leanne."

"I'd like that," Leanne smiled. "You have a wonderful place here, Olivia."

"You can see over it when you come," Olivia promised.

"We'll look forward to that." Carlo took a step forward to kiss Olivia's cheek. "You can reach us at the house. We're staying with Mama and Pappa. I must say hello to Jason before I go. He's here?" Carlo turned his head, hair thick and black as a raven's wing, riotous curls and waves of his childhood tamed by smart styling.

"He's around some place," Olivia said, astonished by the unease that suddenly visited her right out of the blue. Not withstanding she managed to keep a smile on her face. "Jason manages Havilah for me. It was my uncle's wish— Jason is nothing if not super-efficient."

"He and Megan no longer together?" Carlo asked carefully. "I don't want to put my foot in it. Jason's a great guy. I always admired him, I'd hate to upset him in any way."

"That girl, that Megan. I never liked her. You know she was after our Carlo before she got her claws into poor Jason," Salvatore confided and got a sharp prod in the back from his wife for his trouble.

"Scusi," he said, giving his wife a shamefaced glance.

"Good night again, Olivia," Mrs. De Luca said, getting a tight rein on her husband. "It was a lovely, lovely party. Our dear Mr. Linfield would be so proud of you."

"Lovely to meet you, Olivia." Leanne waved.

Lovely to meet you, Olivia thought. For some reason she was finding it a little difficult to swallow.

She stood motionless for some moments as if rooted to

the ground. She watched Carlo and his fiancée break away from his parents making towards Jason whose height and elegant outline made him easy to spot.

Unease continued to spiral in the back of Olivia's mind, unease that was as yet unfocused, an unidentified worry. It left her with a shocked feeling, as though someone had tossed her a red-hot coal. She had always liked Carlo De Luca who had wanted to be a doctor since he was about ten-years-old. His fiancée Leanne appeared to be an attractive, intelligent young woman. She hoped they would be very happy together.

So what was wrong? What was puzzling her brain? She pressed her palms together and shut her eyes in an endeavour to close out the glittering scene. Was it what Salvatore had said? Certainly she'd felt some upset and embarrassment, but the mill manager was a kindly man, he hadn't meant to hurt her. Megan hadn't made herself any friends stealing Jason away. Most people condemned her actions, Megan's actions more than Jason's as was always one way of it. Woman was forever the eternal temptress.

A chink of light shafted into Olivia's brain. Her breath almost stopped. The reason for her unease revealed itself like a revelation, as stunning in its way as an apparition. She felt of all things appallingly *guilty*.

Tali had Carlo De Luca's eyes.

In the next moment she went into denial. What was she thinking? If it were true it could ruin many lives. You're imagining it, Olivia, her internal dialogue started up again. Sheer coincidence. The eyes are similar, that's all. Tali's blue eyes glowed right out of her face, so did Carlo's. They were striking against Carlo's Mediterranean skin and his black hair. They weren't Jason's remarkable deep blue, the setting was quite different. Hadn't she pointed that out to Jason never entertaining for a moment this crazy notion.

Tali was Jason's child. What was the matter with her that she should have these bizarre thoughts? She couldn't handle it right now. Neither could she will it away. She hadn't seen Carlo De Luca for nearly seven years. He had gone to stay with relatives in Sydney while he studied for his medical degree. Why should he turn up tonight of all nights? She had hoped for a happy trouble-free night but trouble had arrived in the guise of an old friend.

A terrible anxiety began to beat in Olivia's breast. If she had seen the resemblance—the smile—the dark curls—why hadn't others? Coincidence, that's why, she clung to that. She could be as fanciful in her imaginings as she liked. She could discuss them with no one else. The only other person she could have confided in was Harry and Harry had gone forever.

Except it wasn't her imagination.

She *knew*.

Robyn and her helpers were near exhausted by the end of the evening. Olivia thanked them most sincerely and handed Robyn her cheque with a handsome bonus thrown in.

"You deserve it all, Robyn." Olivia stood in the kitchen while the last of the dishes were cleared away. "I can't thank you enough. Everything went brilliantly. I know Steven had a great time."

"He fell asleep. He's exhausted." Robyn smiled. "That Tali is a trick! You'd swear you were talking to a grown woman. She came in to say good night."

"Yes, she's gone home with Jason's grandmother, Renata."

"Another character," Robyn said. "If Jason's around I'll get him to carry Steven out to the car. He's grown too heavy for me."

Olivia nodded. "A few of the men have stayed to stack all the chairs, Jason will be with them. You'll find him near the marquees. You must be wanting to get away home."

"I'm really grateful to you, Olivia, for giving me the job."

''You certainly earned every penny. There'll be other occasions, Robyn, I'm sure.''

Still in a tumult of emotion Olivia watched Robyn hurry away to find Jason. Robyn was a single mother with a small son. Why wouldn't she hope to meet a good caring man who could make her and her little boy happy? But Robyn was taking a huge risk allowing herself to fall in love with Jason Corey. Jason was still enmeshed in his past.

As was she. Tonight of all nights Olivia thought they could never erase it.

Long after everyone had gone home and Grace had retired tired out and happy, Olivia sat on the cushioned porch swing, pushing herself back and forth with the toe of one sandalled foot. She knew she wouldn't sleep. She felt overwound to a degree that was truly upsetting. She needed quiet. She needed time to think. Though her thoughts continued to run as inner debates she knew beyond a scintilla of doubt Tali's resemblance to Carlo De Luca was such she had to be a blood relative.

Daughter? Salvatore had divulged Megan had been ''after Carlo before she got her claws into Jason.'' Was that the truth or something Salvatore imagined at the time? All the girls were after his handsome son? Maybe Bella De Luca had been aware of it, too? She certainly gave her husband a powerful prod in the back to shut him up. Most probably so Salvatore wouldn't cause any further embarrassment to his hostess who had been so publicly jilted.

Recognition had presented Olivia with a monumental problem. What was she do? How was she to act? Where did her duty lie? It was an ethical dilemma. Should she try to extract information from Carlo without raising his suspicions. What was she supposed to say? Did you have a sexual relationship with Megan Duffy? She could imagine how he'd react.

What business is it of yours, Olivia?

She'd been about to marry Jason when Megan Duffy came to him and told him she was carrying his baby. She wasn't. She was carrying another man's child, one she mightn't have found so easy to get to marry her. Carlo was set to embark on his life's ambition to become a doctor. His parents had worked so hard to make it happen, nothing and no one could be allowed to stand in the way.

Certainly not a young wife and baby.

That case could be argued. Did her own sufferings and a shattered life give her the right to come forward with her suspicions, Olivia agonized. In doing so she risked bringing down more suffering on other people's heads Then her mind spun round to focusing on Carlo's rights. Didn't Carlo have the right to know he had a child? Didn't his parents—grandparents—have the right to be told they had a grandchild they didn't know about? Closer to home, shouldn't Jason know Tali's wasn't his? And what of Tali? Of Renata? Tali had Italian blood and it showed, but it was De Luca blood that ran through her veins. If I'm right about Tali's true identity and it became public many lives would be turned upside down, Olivia thought wretchedly. Megan was the one who would know. Devious little Megan. How she and Jason had misread her.

But was it her role to sort out the deception? If indeed it was ever to be sorted out. The happiness and well being of a small child was at stake. Bubbly little Tali who adored Jason. How could she possibly destroy that precious relationship? But what would Carlo De Luca do if he ever came to know Tali Corey was his? It seemed certain Megan had never told Carlo she'd fallen pregnant. Megan must have decided what she was going to do when Jason literally fell into her arms.

As she swung back and forth in some agitation Olivia came to the conclusion there was nothing else for her to do but keep her counsel. There was always the possibility Jason when he spoke to Carlo tonight was visited by the same revelation that had poleaxed her.

Tali wasn't his daughter. Megan had lied to him.

It almost seemed like she was waiting for him. Jason mounted the steps that led to the front terrace pausing at the top, one arm outthrust as he leaned against a vine wreathed column for support.

"I'd have thought you'd be longing to turn in. It's been a long night."

"I'm very wakeful." She stared across at him, poised so nonchalantly. His eyes in the porch lights were a blazing sapphire, those same lights drawing out the flames in his dark red hair. He looked perfectly relaxed. Obviously he'd seen nothing disturbing in Carlo's appearance. Her underlying fear ceased to exist. Tali was Jason's daughter. Nothing was going to change that.

None so blind as those who had no wish to see.

"Mind if I join you?" His smile mocked.

Didn't she long for him to join her even if she wasn't about to let him know. "Okay. For a little while." She moved along the cushion, making room for him. Once this had been a favourite place, swinging gently back and forth in the perfumed shadows, the scent of gardenias all around them, the sky studded with a billion diamonds, Harry gone off to bed. Just the two of them. He pulling her across his lap, his warm mouth finding hers, his free hand caressing her breast, the smooth length of her leg, beneath her raised skirt.

His love had empowered them both.

"You're very serious tonight?" He dipped his head so he could stare into her face.

"I'm a serious person."

"I accept that. Only something extra is on your mind. What?"

She shook her head. "Nothing at all."

"All right, so you're not going to tell me." He rested back, the hand nearest her fingering the silk hem of her skirt. "I love this dress. It reminds me of a field of scarlet poppies—red looks beautiful on you."

"Thank you. You're beautiful, too, Jason, as I discovered to my cost."

"Don't tip the bucket of ice over me, Liv," he implored, dropping the hem of her skirt.

"No. Bitterness is not my true nature. What did you think of Carlo and his fiancée?" she asked, turning her head to look at him.

"She's nice, I liked her. Steady, no-nonsense, intelligent. She'll be good for Carlo. He's matured a lot. His becoming a doctor would see to that, but he was a tad wild when he was growing up."

"I don't remember that." Olivia was surprised.

"Liv, you weren't one of the boys. Or one of the girls for that matter. Harry Linfield's beautiful niece lived in a different world. Carlo was a bit of a heartbreaker in his younger days."

"I thought you were that," she said with heavy irony.

He shook his head. "I wouldn't choose to be described like that. I didn't make it my business to check out every girl in town. I had you. I always had you. I never saw anyone else. All I'm saying is Carlo, like plenty of other guys, had a bit of a problem with his sex drive. I'm sure he's settled down. They both looked very happy. They said you'd invited them over for before they go home?"

She nodded. "A small dinner party. I'll get Robyn to cater it. She would appreciate the money—it can't be all that easy for her."

Jason shrugged. "Like I said she has guts. Are you going to tell me now, or save it? Am I invited?"

"Inviting you might be a mistake."

"In what way? I can carry on a decent dinner party conversation. Is it because I'm an employee?"

"Oh, don't be ridiculous!" She was genuinely disgusted. "It's because having you at the dinner table would stir up too many memories. As far as that goes right now you're too close for comfort."

With great exaggeration he inched away. "Better?" He leaned back, so handsome, so dynamic, stretching out his long legs. "I wouldn't have put you down for a coward, Liv."

"You don't believe the sentence must fit the crime?" she asked. "I expected love and loyalty from you, Jason. You got it from me. I still care about you. That's my sentence. If I could do something about it, I would."

"Except neither of us can overlook what was a deeply loving relationship. Love is pain. Love is loss. There's no real life without it. You must know that. I didn't work on a plan to seduce Megan—or any other girl including you— it's not my style. All I can remember about my unpremeditated one-night stand was a spectacular headache that went on for days."

"You shared the same bed after you were married," she said, feeling intensely upset her Jason had probably made love to Megan Duffy many many times. They were married after all, damn it!

Jason sighed deeply. "I tried, Olivia. I had to try, but trying didn't help at all. Having sex with someone you don't love is my idea of misery. I felt sorry for Megan, I still do, she's a troubled soul. After she gave birth to Tali was the worst time of all. You can't know! Her doctor didn't diagnose postnatal depression which had been my fear. It was much more like Megan simply didn't want the responsibility of a child, she didn't want to be tied down. She even resented my love for my own child. Instead of focusing on *my* sins, Liv, you might try to get a handle on your own. Other women can bring themselves to forgive."

"Under circumstances as bad as ours?" She held up her ringless hands.

"That's up to you, Liv." He gathered himself, rose to his impressive height, looking down at her. "I'll say good night." He moved with the long familiar gait across the colonnaded porch and down the steps, walking briskly as though he couldn't get away from her fast enough.

"Hey, come back!"

She scrambled up after him as he strode off into the darkness Why oh why did she send him on his way when she craved his love and attention? Because she kept telling herself it wouldn't work. She could see why she'd avoided commitment with other men. She would never get over Jason.

She chased him across the springy grass, thinking she would never catch him. "Jason!"

He ignored her. Most of the house lights had been turned off as had all the fairy lights in the trees. Only the huge full moon burned a bright orange turning the extensive areas of lawn into lakes of copper.

"Jason?" she cried out again in protest.

"Go to bed, Liv," he called back, increasing his long-legged stride.

"No, I will not! I will not have you walk away from me," she fumed.

He turned suddenly and she broke into a run the scarlet silk of her skirt billowing like wings. Why should he torment her?

"Blast!" Her body juddered to a stop as a pain shot through her foot. She'd run into some obstacle sticking out of the ground. She could feel herself pitching forward, putting out a hand to save herself. She landed harmlessly on the soft grass, hoping she hadn't snagged the silk of her expensive dress.

Jason was beside her, dropping down onto his haunches. "That's the trouble with running in high heels. Are you okay?"

"No, I'm not okay," she said indignantly. "I'm sprawled out on the grass. What in the world did I trip over?"

He peered around the semidarkness. A lacy pattern of light spilled through the open branches of the tree above them. Waves of fragrant frangipani blossom were coming at him. Memories stirred…he and Olivia alone in the enveloping darkness of Havilah's beautiful garden.

"Hard to say." He managed to speak casually. "Probably an exposed root from the tree. Want me to help you up?" He extended an arm.

"Do I look like I'm going to spend the night on the lawn?" she retorted, putting up her hand.

"You wouldn't have to be on your own."

He said it in such a way a great spurt of excitement broke through all her practised reserve. He brought her up in one smooth movement, holding her body close to his. "I have you," he murmured, lowering his head.

There was no refusing his mouth. Those sweet honeyed deeply questing kisses. The unforgettable magic of them. She let herself be enticed, her hunger for him growing. There was no drawing back. The flames of desire needed no fanning, they leapt into the night sky enveloping them in heat. Her whole body flushed as his hands moved slowly over her shoulders and across her back, down to her buttocks, taut beneath the scarlet silk.

He pushed her lustrous cascade of hair aside as he sought the hidden zipper of her dress.

"I love this dress," he murmured. "I'd love it even better if it was lying on the grass." He flipped the thin straps from her shoulders, smoothing, caressing her heated skin. Gradually he moved his lips to her collar bone, the creamy flesh like satin. "I can't go another day, another night without you, Liv." He took her breasts in his hands palming their tender weight. "Let me love you, as I want to. Don't be sad and bitter. I've been punished."

His tongue found its way into her mouth, gently probing, flickering, coaxing hers into a sensual mating dance.

She was very near tears at this insistent sexual teasing. "What are you saying, Jason?" She swallowed, started again, wracked by anxieties and indecisions. "You want us to start over?"

"Yes!" His tone was urgent, heartfelt. "Haven't we both suffered enough? I want you back, Liv."

Her heart was hammering, not just with physical excitement but emotional trauma, too. What was she to do? Let him take her to bed? Her yearning was insatiable enough, but then a pang hit her. In surrendering to Jason she could be destroying her last defence. It could be a perilous mistake. She had worked hard to remove herself to a safe distance. She'd launched herself on a career. Now she was back within his magnetic orbit, her body betraying her at his every touch.

Was it really possible to get back to what they had?

Her body arched, shaking with the effort of pulling away. The fantasy was over. The halcyon days, the days of innocence, would never come again. Megan Duffy had changed everything, coming between them, producing a child. It was fear of the implications of that complicated situation as much as Jason's power over her that made her say, "So you'd have me *and* Havilah to sweeten the marriage deal?" She smiled at him strangely. "Some might call that the perfect arrangement!"

The cold contempt in his voice seared her. "Is *that* what you think?"

"I'm older and wiser now, Jason." She was amazed at how controlled her voice sounded.

"I know what you are." Severity tightened his handsome features. "Wisdom has nothing to do with it. You're a cold, unforgiving, patronising woman. You even enjoy playing the role, Olivia Linfield, arbiter of morals. I don't think you could bring off a future with *anyone* let alone me."

She was hot to the roots of her hair. An answering outrage consumed her. "You're absolutely right! I lived for you once, Jason. It's going to take a little longer than I thought to live without you."

"I'm supposed to take that seriously?" His voice was harsh in his throat. He was angry, very angry. He seized her, kissed her with a fierce, tormented passion like a brand that would stay with her all her life. "What a hypocrite you are. The empty noises you make. I could have you begging in a minute. I could pick you up right now and carry you off to bed. But you know what? You're not worth the trouble. You're stuck in a time warp, Olivia. I'll leave you alone."

Sick at heart she watched him storm off, getting into the estate vehicle and slamming the door hard. She felt as if she'd been caught up in a raging tide, her arms flailing helplessly, her head barely above water. She was doing everything in her power to drive him away yet she couldn't seem to stop herself. She couldn't even begin to analyse her contradictory reactions. The deep secret she had stumbled upon tonight had gone a long way to throw her off balance. How could she possibly start up again with Jason when so many unanswered questions surrounded him?

Olivia started a slow walk back to the house. Despite what Jason believed, it wasn't inconceivable Megan could turn up again. Olivia could almost see her small figure lurking in the shadows. She had to accept now Megan Duffy had probably hated her all along. Olivia had Jason. Olivia had rich Uncle Harry. She lived in a beautiful house. She was loved and admired. All the things that would bring Megan's demons to life. She would be a fool not to face the fact Megan had the potential to cause trouble if she ever got to hear she and Jason were back together again. It now seemed clear the last thing Megan had wanted was for her and Jason to be happy. Megan had demonstrated she was ruthless when it came to self-interest. Megan had blackmailed Jason once and she was quite capable of doing it again secure in the knowledge no one knew her guilty secret.

Olivia dragged herself up onto the porch thinking what a terrible end to a brilliant evening. She had a powerful urge to jump in the car and drive over to Jason's place. She wanted him so much but it had been her own decision to send him away, that cut to the heart. Tears glinted in her eyes. She could still feel the imprint of his mouth on hers, the scent of him was on her skin. All around her was confusion and pain. Above all a frustrated physical yearning that had her stomach cramping. She knew she would be unable to sleep.

I love you, Jason, she said aloud. She had been starved of him for years yet she had sent him away. What mysteries there were at the heart of love.

She was crying openly now.

CHAPTER EIGHT

ROBYN'S KITCHEN was like a picturesque doll's house sitting on the corner of the town's main street. The entire façade was given over to a large bay window displaying a whole range of delectable food stuffs, a narrow glass paned door with a fancy brass door handle for entry. A luxuriant ficus in a glazed pot stood to one side. The area beneath the picture window was made eye catching with a half dozen spectacular bromeliads with dense spikes of scarlet flowers. The whole effect was delightful.

Olivia hesitated a moment longer, admiring, before she pushed open the door, savouring the cold blast of air that greeted her from the air-conditioning. It was a sizzlingly hot day, the humidity high. Robyn in a relaxed-style white uniform with a blue and white gingham apron tied around her waist was busy serving a customer. Olivia overheard an order of miniature quiches, phyllo triangles, a huge aioli platter beautifully arranged, a couple of roulades, some very fancy finger food, obviously there was a party planned—but Robyn gave Olivia a quick welcoming smile as did Robyn's aides, the same women who had come to the house for the Christmas party.

"What about a cup of coffee while you're waiting?" Robyn took a moment out to ask. "Won't be long."

"Lovely." Olivia found herself a high stool in front of a curved niche with a selection of gourmet magazines spread out over it.

Within moments one of Robyn's helpers brought her a cappuccino with a thick crema and the shape of a little fish dusted onto the top. It was accompanied by a tiny home-made pecan pie. Olivia thanked her. They exchanged a few

118

remarks about the weather, the possibility of a late afternoon storm, then Olivia was left alone to enjoy her coffee.

She looked around. Robyn's Kitchen though obviously too small for what appeared to be a burgeoning business had a very pleasant ambience. She had already asked Robyn if she'd trained to be a chef but Robyn had told her she hadn't. Rather she came from a family of good cooks whose interest in food extended well beyond the average. Finding herself in the position of working mother with not a lot of qualifications, she had decided to come north and open a small shop offering home-made provisions using fresh high quality ingredients.

Robyn was to be congratulated on her success, Olivia thought. As Jason had remarked, she was a gutsy lady but Olivia thought she still didn't know the full extent of Robyn's courage and drive.

Ten minutes later Robyn joined her. "How lovely to see you, Olivia. Welcome to my little shop. In a way my haven."

"And you've made something delightful of it." Olivia smiled. "I remember this shop, a Miss Inness ran it for many years. She used to make beautiful little outfits for babies and small children. Lovely work. You used to have to take your shoes off before you came in. One would have thought she had a fancy white carpet that would soil easily, but the floor was tiled just as it is today." Olivia glanced down at the terra cotta tiles. "I think it was all about cleanliness. It seems to me looking around you could do with bigger premises, Robyn?"

Robyn nodded, her expression bright with satisfaction. "I never expected to extend my horizons so quickly. As I told you, business was very slow when I first came here. The town mostly supported their own. Marco and the like. Not that they're not very good, but I felt there was room for competition."

"Fortunately Jason was in a position to help you to spread the word."

"Yes, Jason!" A flush of colour burned through Robyn's skin. "He's an extraordinarily attractive man. People take notice of what he says. He's so kind."

"He can be," Olivia said, finishing the last delicious morsel of the tiny pecan pie.

Robyn looked at Olivia a shade tentatively. "I hope you don't mind, Olivia, but the local people have told me—"

"Jason and I were to be married?" Olivia supplied, realizing Robyn didn't know how best to approach the subject. "It didn't work out. Smart as he is Jason was outmanoeuvred by one Megan Duffy. I'm sure you've heard the rest of the story."

Robyn nodded, looking a little shaken. "He still loves you, you know. I'd give anything to have a man like Jason Corey love me," she added with sudden intensity.

"What makes you think he still loves me," Olivia asked, very quietly.

"I knew the moment I saw you together," Robyn said in a slightly elegiac tone. "Now I know not to make the big mistake of trying to get him to notice me."

"Oh, Robyn!" Olivia groaned. "Is that what you want?"

"Aren't I crazy?" Robyn grimaced. "I see now it was just a daydream."

"I don't know what to say." Olivia wanted to console Robyn, give her something positive to hold on to but she knew she couldn't. A miracle might still happen. Jason might get around to marrying his first love.

"That's okay." Robyn smiled and patted Olivia's hand. "I'll settle for friendship. Jason is a good man. He's a wonderful father to Tali."

"Yes, he is." Olivia dipped her shiny dark head. "Please stop me if you don't want to talk about it. Your marriage, I take it, it was unhappy?"

Robyn fixed her golden-brown eyes on a point just past

Olivia's shoulder. "It was much worse than that, Olivia. It was violent, black eyes and broken bones. I stood it as long as I could, until he threatened me with a knife, cut my face." She touched her cheek gingerly as though it still bled. "I found the courage to call the police after that. I'd told no-one about Lyle. Not my parents, my brother or what few friends I had left. I was too ashamed. I kept up the pretence our marriage was happy, a lot of people thought it was. Lyle was a different person when we were out. He changed the moment we stepped in the door. The truth was I was a real mess. I needed help."

"How awful! I'm terribly, terribly sorry." Olivia felt a sudden despisal of Robyn's husband who had been cruel enough to scar her face. She thought of all the women in life who made not only wrong choices, but life-threatening ones as well. She could never imagine Jason in any circumstances raising his hand to a woman. "How did you manage to get away?" she asked gently.

"My parents took us in," Robyn said. "I couldn't lie or pretend anymore. It was all out in the open. My husband beat me. When my brother found out he was livid. He warned Lyle not to come near me again. It worked for a while but I decided I had to go. I couldn't have my family living with such upset. Eight months ago I found out I no longer had to fear Lyle's coming after me. He was killed in an on-site industrial accident. I have no husband—Stevie has no father. It's especially sad because Steven misses his father. Lyle never directed his anger and frustration at our son."

"Thank God for that!" Olivia shuddered. "Thank you for confiding in me, Robyn. Life hasn't been easy for you, but I'd like to take a hand in seeing things pick up. Actually what I'm here for is to ask you to cater a dinner party I'm giving this coming Saturday. An old friend is in town with his fiancée—Carlo De Luca—his father manages the mill. I've had a bit of a brainwave while we've been sitting here.

I'd like you, if you can manage it all, to sit down to dinner with us as a guest. You'd be doing me a favour making up the numbers.''

Robyn looked dubious about that, but flattered and pleased as well. She began to beam. ''I think you're being kind to me, Olivia.''

''I think you'll enjoy it.'' Olivia had thought of someone who would get along with Robyn just fine. ''If you can work out a menu and let me have it as soon as possible that would be great. What I have in mind is for you to supervise up to a point and your helpers can do the rest, dish the meal up and serve it. Grace won't be there as she likes spending Christmas and New Year with her widowed sister in Brisbane. Does that appeal to you? Dress up. Chance to look good.''

''I don't know what to say.'' Robyn could barely contain her pleasure.

Olivia laughed. ''That's easy. Say yes.''

I'm only half living, Megan thought, flinging herself down on the unmade bed in the trailer. It's all just too bloody much, working in a supermarket, living in a dirty run-down trailer in a caravan park. She'd have been much better off staying with Jason and the kid. Jason might never love her, might never yearn after her like Princess Bloody Olivia, but he'd tried hard to be a friend to her. In his own way he cared about her but he couldn't love her like he loved his perfect Olivia or naughty little Natalie who so often put her in a rage. It was sad really when Tali wasn't Jason's kid.

All these years later she really couldn't get over the fact Jason on the eve of marrying his precious princess had believed the trumped-up story she sold him about him being the father of her unborn child. Sometimes she felt really really sorry she had done that to Jason. Other times she laughed so hard it gave her a stitch. She knew if she'd gone to Carlo he could have told her to get lost; get an abortion, or so she thought.

Carlo De Luca was dead set on becoming a doctor. A big career move. Prestige, money. Megan being Megan didn't think it had a lot to do with helping people. Carlo in her view surely wasn't going to help pathetic little Megan Duffy who he'd only made love to because he needed sex and his best girl Jennifer had gone on a trip with her parents. Jason's darling little Tali, the child he'd been so protective of, had been conceived in the back seat of Carlo De Luca's second hand car.

Megan rolled her eyes at the memory. Carlo came so quick—two minutes—she barely had time to feel anything, let alone conceive a child, a child she never wanted. She didn't want to take care of any kid, feed her, bathe her, clean up after the mess. She didn't want to be turned into a child minder. She didn't want a naughty kid that shouted and glowered at her and yelled for her daddy. Not every woman wanted kids. Why couldn't people understand that? She swore after Tali she'd never get pregnant again.

First and foremost she had to look after herself, which was why she had to get out of this dirty trailer. She'd seen what had happened at Sean's party, the way Gordon Cassidy had spiked Jason's drink. Sean's half-witted friends thought it a great joke. Sean's gang had a hero-hate relationship going on with Jason Corey who was everything none of them could ever be. Not only that Jason was going to marry Princess Bloody Linfield and shift out of a crummy bungalow into a mansion.

It was great, great fun for them to see Jason fall under the influence of the drug though Jason was so fit and strong it took a surprising amount of time.

But she had waited. And waited. She didn't want to do it but she knew she would. She'd had a massive crush on Jason Corey since she was twelve years old. He was so handsome, so much the gentleman, so clever, so totally bloody nice. He was the total opposite to her fool of a brother with no money, no job. Jason was only being kind coming to Sean's party. Sean had actually been thrilled about it, but he didn't take good care of his hero. Sean knew what was going on. He let it happen, though he was sorry about it the next day.

Too late! When Jason came to the next morning she was snuggling up naked beside him. It was wonderful just lying against him. He had the most marvellous body, so fit and toned. Yet she'd had no qualms about allowing him to believe he had made drunken love to her during the night. He was so hung over he finally concluded he must have. Not many people knew it but she was an unbelievably good actress when she was certain she was pregnant she convinced herself she didn't have a choice. Carlo De Luca would rant and rage—Carlo's mother would shout abuse at her, accuse her of lying—Carlo's mother was formidable with a spectacular temper. She had a lot better chance of fooling the honourable Jason, Jason who'd actually believed she was a virgin. Not that she ever let just anyone mess with her. She chose who she got into a car with. She knew she had to be very discreet or her father would come after her with his fists.

A week ago, quite by accident, she'd picked up an old newspaper with a small snapshot of a face she knew well on the front page and underneath the caption Harry Linfield Dies, Story Page 5. Towards the back she'd found the obituary and more pictures. Harry Linfield had been a big man in North Queensland—they even knew him in the Territory. She'd ripped the page out after she'd devoured the contents. Now she dug it up again from under the thin mattress. How she hated living like this! It had been all right for a while but now she and Brucie, the guy she was shacked up with, no drop-dead dreamy hunk like Jason, were arguing all the time.

Damn! if Princess Olivia hadn't inherited all her uncle's

money and the sugar plantation, too—historic Havilah. There was a picture of her standing in front of that magnificent old colonial mansion. Olivia with the long black hair and the diamond-coloured eyes looking so beautiful and posh. It had never crossed Olivia's saintly mind she had hated her. Taking Jason off Olivia Linfield hadn't made her sad…there was no-one she'd rather have done it to. Quite a coup stealing the bridegroom! Teach Olivia a lesson! Why should she be rich and beautiful and happy when Megan Duffy—she'd never really thought of herself as Jason's wife, Megan Corey—had so many needs that could never be filled. Olivia Linfield had been lucky enough to be born into wealth and privilege. Why then should she be allowed to marry her prince? No, she hadn't felt bad about betraying her lovely, kind friend who had deigned to ask her to be bridesmaid. The privileged loved doing good deeds. Then they didn't feel so bad about having so much more than anyone else.

Now and again Megan was seized by regret for what she had done, but only to Jason. She had really believed once they were married she could get him to love her.

It had never happened. Instead he had loved Tali who looked at her with Carlo De Luca's eyes. Jason would do anything to keep that kid. Maybe it was time to pay him and his true love, Olivia, a visit. She'd known for some time Jason had gone back home to be with his dying mother. She knew Harry Linfield had given Jason the job of overseer on Havilah. Harry Linfield had loved the guy! It was on the cards Linfield had left Jason a little something in his will.

All in all Harry Linfield's dying had presented a great opportunity she'd just have to take. If Jason wanted to keep custody of Tali he'd have to pay.

A lot of money!

Poor Jason! But then Princess Olivia was back on the scene to help him.

*   *   *

When he opened the door Jason was startled to find Olivia hand in hand with Tali, standing on the porch.

"Daddy!" Tali flung herself at him, thrilled although she was a big girl, he still picked her up like when she was little. He was so strong!

"Sweetheart, I was coming for you," he said. "I needed a quick shower first."

Tali snuggled up to him, "You smell nice. Your hair is all wet." She reached up to tug at his dark red plume of hair. "Livvy drove me home. I've had a lovely time. Livvy let me look through lots of family photographs. There were lots of you. Lots of you and Livvy. You looked lovely, really sweet. That was before you were going to be married."

"Are you coming in, Olivia?" Jason asked, setting Tali on her feet.

"Just for a minute." Their estrangement had gone on for days, disturbing her more than she was prepared to admit. "I need to talk to you about something."

"Really?" Her presence affected him powerfully but he kept his voice and his expression cool. "Couldn't it wait until I got up to the house? Or is the house out of bounds?"

"Don't be like that, Jason," she said quietly, the tiniest throb of emotion in the tone.

Tali ran ahead, while Jason stood back for Olivia to precede him. "I'm in time to watch my show!" Tali called gleefully, making a bee-line for the television.

"Watch it in your room, sweetheart, so Olivia and I can talk."

"Sure!" Tali bestowed on them both a breezy smile. Her second tooth was coming down fast, closing the endearing gap. "Sing out when you're going, Livvy. I'll come and wave you off."

"I should think so," Olivia rejoined.

"So what do you want to talk to me about?" Jason asked,

raking a hand through the thick damp hair Tali's fingers had disturbed.

"I need to know if you're coming to the dinner party on Saturday?"

She had left her hair loose and it was swirling around her bare shoulders. She was wearing a white flower printed dress with a halter neckline he had never seen before. She looked beautiful, cool as a lily when waves of heat were breaking over him. "Obviously you need me to make up the numbers," he clipped off.

She shook her head. "There are any number of people I can ask as you well know."

He half turned away from her. "Thank you for minding Tali. I hope she behaved well?"

"Better than you," Olivia said. "You've gone out of your way to avoid me and I'm supposed to be your boss."

"Well you aren't," he said flatly.

"I am. Believe me." Her eyes turned stormy.

"I know." He suddenly laughed. "But I'm having second thoughts about staying."

She couldn't control her shock. "You have to stay, it was Harry's wish. Besides I need you."

"Oh, sorry, I didn't realize." He piled on the sarcasm. "Is there a dress code for this glamorous evening, or are jeans an option?"

She stared up at him, naked vulnerability in her eyes. "Oh, Jason, can't we start again?"

"I thought you'd made it perfectly plain that's the last thing you want."

"Well, I'm trying," she breathed. "I've asked Ben Riley."

There was a wealth of mockery in his tone. "Big deal!"

"I thought Ben and Robyn might get on like a house on fire?" she explained.

His sapphire eyes turned to her. "Matchmaking, are we?"

"I think Robyn would like to remarry," she answered.

"A good man this time, one who'll look after her and her little boy."

"Great! I just happen to agree with you. Do you think you'll ever find a man you want, Olivia? It's not going to be easy. You have impossibly high standards."

"I can't have," she pointed out with a mix of bitter-sweetness. "I wanted you, Jason."

His blue eyes glittered, jewel-like against his copper skin. "I flatter myself a little bit you still want me," he taunted. "Just for sex."

"Which we haven't had! Please keep your voice down. Tali might hear you."

His mouth twitched. "Tali has the television on so loud she wouldn't hear a police siren inside the house."

Olivia looked at him in exasperation. "Could you please tell me if you're coming or not?"

"Would you be infuriated if I didn't?" Some devil in him was urging him on.

"Yes," she returned bluntly.

"I get it. It's not an invitation, it's a royal command."

Olivia turned about so quickly her short skirt flared out around her long legs. "I've got a list of who's coming in the car." She tossed at him over her shoulder. "If you can bear to walk out with me, I'll give it to you."

"I'm dying to know," he said in a drawl like dark honey. "Hang on a minute, Olivia," he abruptly chided. "Who have you invited for me?"

She spun about, eyes brilliant. She felt like rushing at him and hitting him. Instead she said, "What about me?"

"Hell, girl, when you feel the way you do?" He swaggered back on his booted heels.

"It's only for one night."

"I see." He smiled lazily. "That's okay then. We can be polite for a few hours. Now, are you going to let Tali know you're leaving, or stomp off?"

"I'm sure Harry didn't put up with any of this?" she said, holding tight on her temper.

"Harry definitely wasn't you. Females don't always make the best bosses."

"At least I haven't sacked you," she said sharply. "If we could get back to Saturday. Tali could stay overnight with Renata but I've been thinking I could easily make her comfortable upstairs. I know how much Renata loves Tali but Tali can be a handful."

"Whyever would you be telling me?" he asked incredulously, following Olivia to the door. "I know the child, she's my daughter." Jason turned his head and called loudly. "Tali, Olivia is leaving. Tali!"

CHAPTER NINE

TEN in all sat down to dinner. As it had promised to be a beautiful summer night without threat of a late afternoon storm, Olivia had debated using the loggia instead of the formal dining room but in the end the formal dining room had won out.

"I love it. It's magic!" Carlo's fiancée, Leanne, looked around her in open admiration. Havilah homestead was quite something she considered, certainly the grandest house she'd even been into in her life. The large high ceilinged room was painted a pale duck-egg blue with a pristine white trim, and there were many touches of gilt in the elegant plaster work on the ceiling, the sumptuous frames of the beautiful paintings and the circular mirror—obviously a valuable antique—that hung above a console supported by two gilded nymphs.

A large, very beautiful cut-glass chandelier again in the antique style with sparkling festoons and pedant drops was suspended above centre table. Two tall narrow glass vases, topped by many sprigs of delicate white butterfly orchids with yellow and rose centres, flanked a lovely big blue and white centrepiece decorated with little figures—Leanne thought were called putti—the large bowl atop the pillared stand was a mass of lovely white rosebuds. Four silver candlesticks—they looked like solid silver—with tall golden candles completed the entrancing setting. Olivia had gone to a lot of trouble for her guests. The cream brocade cloth with its matching napkins looked too beautiful to be used. Leanne hoped she wouldn't spill a drop of wine in all the excitement. The crystal sparkled, the silver gleamed, the fine bone china was a lustrous white with an exquisite blue, jade and gold decoration

Leanne soaked it all in, thrilled she had been given the opportunity to visit. She wanted to catch this scene and hold it for all time. So much of her life had been spent in study. When she and Carlo were married she thought she might branch out into a hostess who could set a stylish and elegant dinner table though she didn't aspire to match this sumptuous formality.

As hostess Olivia sat at one end of the long table. She'd wanted to seat Jason at the other end but knew she couldn't. Instead she chose Ben Riley. Ben universally described as "a lovely man" was tall, well built, in his early forties with attractive irregular features, a thick thatch of brown hair and intelligent dark eyes. Ben's late father, Keith Riley, another plantation owner, had been close friends with Harry. Ben had inherited his father's expansive estate but tragedy had marred Ben's life. His young wife, Victoria, a scant two years into the marriage, after a routine medical examination was found to be suffering from a rare cancer that took her almost overnight. The shock to both families and everyone who loved her had been great.

That was close on twelve years ago, Olivia recalled, Ben had never remarried. His beloved Victoria had not faded easily from his mind. Olivia understood, but still thought it sad because Ben had so much to offer a woman and he truly deserved happiness himself. Children. Heirs. Olivia hoped with all her heart Ben and Robyn would be attracted.

Robyn looked her very best tonight in a classic little black dress that showed off her smooth, even tan and her good figure. She wore a more dramatic evening make-up than her usual light touch, several coats of mascara that accentuated her soulful dark eyes, her cap of blond hair gelled into a quirky, sophisticated style. Olivia hadn't wanted either one of them to feel she was pushing them together so she hadn't seated Robyn beside Ben, but not too far away, either.

She and Robyn had worked hard for most of the afternoon getting everything in order. Olivia had taken charge of the table setting and the various flower arrangements which were lavish and beautiful. Olivia had a passion for flowers; a passion she had shared with Harry. One of her trademarks a friend once told her was the lovely arrangement of seasonal flowers that always adorned the console in her apartment's small entrance hall to greet visitors.

Robyn had given her full attention to matters of the kitchen. As she was to sit down as a guest she and her helpers had prepared as much of the food as they could ahead of time. It would make for a smooth performance. Robyn was delighted with Olivia's table setting, applauding the fact Olivia didn't have the slightest qualm about pulling out the family heirlooms. The centrepiece, for instance, was exquisite. "Much loved and much used," Olivia had told her. Robyn was certain it was very valuable.

For a starter they had decided on something delectable but easy. Oysters with Lebanese cucumber salad served in the shucked shells. As a backup in case some of the guests didn't like oysters, seared scallops with a white truffle butter and a little fresh fettucine as a garnish. The seafood of the region was superb, the tropical climate called for something light so they kept to seafood for the mains; slow baked fillets of barramundi with a creamy crab sauce and asparagus.

For dessert there was a choice of little lemon curd tarts with fresh berries and cream or a combination of Havilah's latest exotic fruits macerated in marsala brown sugar and orange juice, reduced to a sauce then served with mascarpone. Olivia had had a pretaste and thought it marvellous. The wines came from Havilah's well stocked cellar. Harry had been quite a wine-buff, the premier wines stored at the correct temperature.

Everyone with the exception of Leanne and Robyn knew

everyone else. All were of an age. Mostly they had gone to primary school together. Two of the female guests, Lucy and Tamara, both since married to their long-time boy-friends were to have been Olivia's bridesmaids. Neither showed the merest glimmer of animosity towards Jason who had broken their friend, Olivia's heart. Jason appeared to have been well and truly forgiven. In fact Olivia's single friend, Candice was openly flirting with him when Lucy wasn't busy chattering away to him.

Without even trying Jason became the pivotal guest around whom most of the laughter and conversation eddied. Jason had his grandmother's flare for telling a good story Olivia thought. She allowed her eyes to rest on him, think-ing nothing could destroy the bond between them for all the long years of alienation. She loved him. She would always love him but she couldn't rid herself of the melancholy for what might have been. The wasted years!

He looked terrific. Handsome, dynamic, his colouring a striking contrast of deep blue eyes and hair like dark flame. He was wearing a great outfit as well. That was the Italian in him; the bella figura. His cream linen jacket was so finely woven the fabric looked like silk; an open-necked deep blue dress shirt, cream slacks. Clothes hung well on him. He had the body of the classic athlete, perfectly shaped and kept that way by his hard working outdoor life. Once started, it was hard indeed to take her eyes off him but at least she had the excuse he was in her field of vision.

Jason! she brooded. My heartache and my desire!

They were all laughing heartily at some story he was telling about a massive salt water crocodile that had dis-rupted the peace of a camp barbeque he'd been invited to on a Territory cattle station. Crocodiles were like people they liked to go walkabout. Olivia would never in a lifetime consider taking a dip in a lagoon or a river north of Capricorn, but she'd known more than a few cases of fool-hardy visitors to the region—mostly males from the other side of the world—who'd chosen to ignore all the warnings and never lived to return home.

It was good to see Ben easing back into a social life, obviously enjoying himself, his dark head turning often in Robyn's direction to gauge her reactions, the way she responded to a story he particularly enjoyed. A shared sense of humour was important. Unlike Renata, Jason didn't garnish his stories with outrageous fibs or flights of extravagant fancy just the quirks of a brilliant sense of humour.

Laughter swelled around the table. The evening was turning out to be a great success. Leanne in her pleasure and excitement grabbed Carlo's hand, holding it to her cheek.

The delicious food was eaten. ''These oysters are superb!'' ''Oooh this barramundi!'' Wineglasses were emptied and refilled. They had started dinner by all leaning closer to each other, clinking champagne glasses and ceremoniously toasting: ''Carlo and Leanne!''

The love between the engaged couple was palpable. Olivia was pleased to see the volatile Carlo she remembered had matured greatly. He spoke well and movingly of his experiences as a young doctor. How would it all turn out if Carlo was ever to learn Tali was his child? Olivia sucked in a settling breath. It was imperative she keep her chaotic thoughts out of her expression. How would the very much in love Leanne react to such a revelation? Would she be unable to accept it? Would she be bitterly upset Carlo's first born would now never be hers but another woman's child? Olivia understood only too well that feeling. She had to face the fact, too, she wouldn't have asked Carlo and his fiancée to dinner had she not issued the invitation before she realized Tali could be Carlo's child. Discovery could irrevocably change lives.

Not that Carlo would have dreamed he had fathered a little daughter. Mega had been utterly cruel and unscrupulous in her actions, probably convincing herself Jason offered her far more than ever Carlo De Luca could. Neither was Bella De Luca, Carlo's mother a woman to lie to. Megan had chosen Jason without giving any consideration to the rights of Tali's biological father, Carlo. Not wanting a child herself Megan would have convinced herself Carlo wouldn't want a child either when both he and Leanne had already told the table they wanted a family.

"At least four!" Leanne announced and blushed while Carlo smiled into her eyes.

But Carlo already had a child. That was not a minor detail but something momentous.

They rose to have coffee and liqueurs out in the loggia overlooking the rear garden. Olivia had asked Havilah's head gardener, Wally, to collect dozens of hibiscus blossoms to float on the turquoise surface of the swimming pool with its myriad reflections of lights from the house. Olivia had taken time to turn on some music, not loud, but gently romantic letting it waft through the house. Upstairs she checked on Tali. The little girl was sleeping deeply and peacefully, two hands tucked beneath her cheek. She looked adorable. Her rounded cheeks were slightly flushed in sleep, her long eyelashes making dark crescents against her skin.

For a moment Olivia's vision wavered with tears. Her suspicions, she knew they were true, had burdened her. A lot of people lived with secrets. Family secrets tended to get locked up more securely than most. Only one day—for however long it took—long buried secrets are let out.

Someone always knew. Someone always kept silent. Many until they were on their death bed, preparing to meet their Maker and anxious to clear the slate. Olivia understood that, she longed to offload her own burden, but she knew that she couldn't. What a difference this innocent child had made to her, to Jason who loved her. And Tali loved Jason. She couldn't possibly do or say anything to threaten that relationship. On the other hand, would good intentions absolve her from all culpability? She knew how the law stood. If Carlo wanted his child and was able to look after her the

courts would take Tali off Jason. That could precipitate a
crisis; destroy the hard-won harmony of so many lives.

She kept going round and around in circles. Carlo was
Tali's father. Salvatore and Bella were Tali's grandparents.
Surely they had a right to know? Olivia realized she was no
latter-day Solomon.

She left the night light glowing softly and gently closed
the door. Jason had assured her Tali could sleep through
anything. The bedroom faced the front of the house anyway.
They wouldn't be disturbing her. It had already been decided Tali would ''sleep over'' as she put it. Tali had become very used to being around Havilah, the homestead and
the estate.

''It's my second house, Livvy,'' she said, touchingly secure in Olivia's constant, calm affection. It was so very
different from Tali's memories of her mother with her angry
moods, the kicking foot, the lashing hand, Tali had learned
very early to scrabble away from.

When Olivia returned to the loggia Jason caught her eye.
She nodded almost imperceptibly, signalling that all was
well with Tali. Neither of them had mentioned Tali was
actually in the house, fast asleep in an upstairs bedroom.
She'd heard Lucy ask after Tali. She supposed Lucy thought
the child was with her grandmother. Everyone had the errant
mother, Megan, at the back of their minds, but no one
wished to confront the situation or speak her name. No one
quite knew either how Jason had been so quickly reinstated
in Olivia's life after their bitter estrangement, but Olivia
could see the possibility of their coming together again had
backing from all sides.

Quite simply everyone chose to believe Megan Duffy had
been an aberration. Lucy for one had never liked her. In the
intervening years Lucy had often passed the remark if only
Olivia had listened to her the whole sorry mess would never
have happened.

But the sorry mess had borne fruit. There was Tali, so

precious and innocent. At six already a character. Small wonder Olivia was in a state of deep confusion. She had to keep to herself—that was the hard part. If only she could have spoken quietly to Harry. All through her childhood and adolescence Harry had been there to dispense wisdom. Even Harry would be hard pressed to come up with a working solution to this ethical problem.

Fate was ordained. It was never to be denied. All evening it had sat at their table, an invisible guest, then a short time before the party broke up it materialized. They were standing in the entrance hall saying their goodbyes, when suddenly and without warning Tali came racing along the gallery and down the staircase making a big lunge for Jason who caught her up in his arms.

"Sweetheart, what's the matter?" he asked in concern.

Tali snuggled her head against his shoulder. "I had a bad dream, Daddy."

"There, there." He soothed her by running a hand through her riotous glossy curls. "You're okay now, baby. Daddy's here." Jason turned his head to the others. "This, guys, is my little daughter, Natalie. Tali, for short. Say hello, Tali, if you can."

Tali made a funny little gurgling sound in her throat, then lifted her head, her blue eyes like saucers. "Hi guys!" she said, producing a captivating grin.

"How are you doing, Tali?" Lucy took the child's hand and kissed it. "How lovely to see you."

The others moved in to make a fuss of the child whose appearance was so absolutely unexpected.

Only Olivia and Carlo kept their distance.

Even from where she was standing Olivia heard Carlo's rasping intake of breath as though the air was being dragged two ways, into his lungs and upwards to his brain.

He's recognised her, Olivia thought. Her heart quickened.

The fine hairs at her nape and her temples tingled. In a second pandemonium could break loose.

"Carlo?" Leanne turned a smiling face to her fiancé, holding out her hand. "Come say hello to Tali."

Carlo continued to stand as though rooted to the spot, though Olivia could see he was steadying himself with one hand on the side of a chair.

Olivia steeled herself for what she felt would surely come. A fiery emotional outburst, with Carlo's Latin blood coming to the fore. A demand for answers. Instead Carlo gathered himself, moving in to join the small group. "Well, Tali, I'd have hated to have gone away without meeting you," he said, lifting a hand and drawing a gentle finger down Tali's petalled cheek.

The nerves in Olivia's stomach were fluttering so badly she thought she'd be sick. Softly as the words were spoken they seemed to her to carry a real note of foreboding.

"Hello, Mr. Carlo," Tali responded with a big smile, making a grab for Carlo's hand and holding it.

"Hello, Natalie." Carlo made no attempt to withdrawn his hand. He continued to stare back at the child as though this was just between the two of them. "What a pretty girl you are!" A powerful light had been let into Carlo's shocked and confused brain. All the pieces slotted into place. This child was deeply familiar to him—he knew her face, he knew her manner, the sweet cheeky grin. She was the image of his sister, Gina at the same age. The resemblance leapt at him, so strongly it almost knocked him to the ground.

Surely if he could see it, why couldn't others? Or did people only see what they wanted to see?

Normally Leanne was so quick. Apparently she saw nothing. She had a soft, open smile on her face as did the other women.

His friend Jason continued to hold the child, his strikingly handsome face, so vividly masculine, ineffably tender. Carlo darted another glance around. No one looked troubled. No expression was turning quizzical. They all accepted Natalie was Jason's child. Jason's and Megan Duffy's. Sly, conniving, cheating Megan Duffy who had once given the entire district a great performance as a coy little virgin. In Carlo's opinion, Megan was the worst Duffy of them all.

The beautiful Olivia, so perfectly right in this mansion, hovered in the background. Her face was as still as a porcelain statue, devoid of expression, but her eyes glittered with some emotion Carlo identified as trepidation. Olivia was waiting for the time-bomb to go off.

Olivia *knew*. He had real conviction without knowing exactly why. Olivia was a smart woman, part of the triangle. Olivia had fathomed the mystery. She should have been wild with anger at what had been done to her, but he could see not anger, but overwhelming sorrow in her eyes, anxiety for Jason and the child, possibly him. Olivia Linfield, like her late uncle had a kind heart. Not that it had done her much good.

The sound of Leanne's voice broke into Carlo's agonised thoughts; split-second timing when he had been ready to snap. "We really should be going, Carlo." She smiled and put her hand on his shoulder. "We're keeping this little lady from her bed."

But Tali was more interested in saying something else to Carlo, who had obviously caught and held her attention. "Am I going to see you again, Mr. Carlo?" she asked, looking as though she hoped he'd say yes.

"Why don't you ask your father?" Carlo looked with intensity into Jason's eyes, but Jason appeared to notice nothing unusual.

"Why don't you ask him?" Tali promptly replied.

"Hey what is all this about?" Jason laughed. "You've charmed my little daughter, Carlo."

"I guess so," Carlo murmured, moving his gaze to where Olivia stood.

Olivia knew what that instant rapport meant.

Love at first sight. That's what happened when a man first laid eyes on his firstborn.

"That went off particularly well," Jason remarked as he carried a hugely yawning Tali up the stairs. "I was pleasantly surprised—I'm not sure why—how nice Carlo was to Tali. They really clicked. The Carlo I remember didn't find kids so appealing. Now I'm thinking he'll make a good father."

Olivia breathed a cautious, "Yes."

Tali was already asleep by the time Jason tucked her in. He bent his auburn head to drop a kiss on her temple. "She told me she was dreaming about her mummy. It's sad that has to fall into the bad dream category."

"Whatever did Megan do to her, Jason?" Olivia asked when they were back in the softly lit hallway.

He grimaced. "Not Megan. Not now," he pleaded. "I thoroughly enjoyed tonight. It was good to catch up with everyone." Jason glanced down at Olivia quickly, catching her expression.

"What's the matter with you?"

"There's nothing the matter with me." She continued walking along the quiet corridor.

"Standard answer. There is something the matter with you, I know you too well."

"I'm always afraid something is going to go wrong," she admitted quietly.

He was silent for a moment, conscious of her enormous emotional pull. "I think the worst thing that was going to happen to us has already happened, don't you, Liv?"

"As in Megan?" she asked. Her spirit was reeling from all her discoveries.

"Now I'm afraid," he said. "I don't want to talk about Megan. She wreaked an awful lot of damage."

"I don't think you're through with her, either." Olivia

made the unwilling prediction, a shiver passing through her body.

"I told you, Liv. Megan doesn't care about Tali. All her feelings are for herself."

Olivia shook her head. "It might be more complicated than that, Jason. I know Megan thought nothing of causing pain. I've had to accept she probably hated me, interpreting my efforts to be kind as secretly despising her. I never did then, but I do *now*. What if she ever gets to hear you're back on Havilah?" She lifted her head to stare at his chiselled profile. "She made sure she parted us once."

"We can't grieve forever for what was lost, Liv," he told her gently. "Megan can do nothing. She can't and won't take Tali from me."

"You want Tali beyond anything, don't you?" she asked, a sad note in her voice.

"What a question, Liv? She's my daughter. Are you saying I love Tali more than I could ever love you?"

"Do you love me?" she asked, a melancholy note in her voice.

He placed a hand on her shoulder, halting her progress. He made her face him. "I'm not afraid of my own heart, Olivia. I do love you. Sometimes I feel it's beyond my control like it's written in the stars. All these years I've had to bear without you, it was like living with a permanent hunger. When I lost you it was like the end of the world."

"And now?"

He looked deep into her beautiful eyes, seeing in their crystal depths grief, confusion, even remarkably, a hint of fear. "I don't think *you* can forget the past, Liv. You've lost your faith. You've lost your trust. Something happened tonight. I don't know what and you won't tell me. Something you remembered? Something that's frightening you? Can't you tell me?"

"Hold me," she said. "Just hold me," she implored.

He gave an odd choky laugh. "Liv! Do you enjoy torturing me? I can't just hold you, I'm mad for you. I'm a man who desperately wants a woman. Not any woman. You. I don't want to be standing in the hallway holding you around the waist. I want you naked in bed. I haven't forgotten what our extraordinary intimacy was like. I haven't forgotten the absolute rapture. I haven't forgotten how you look and how you sound when you come. I haven't forgotten our lovemaking, Liv. It meant everything in the world to me."

She could have wept. She could have screamed. The one thing she couldn't do was articulate her fears. She fell back on her usual lament. "Then how did you do that to us?"

Immediately the words were out of her mouth, she knew she'd lost him. Yet again. He all but threw her off, taking the steps of the staircase at such a pace he might have been born with winged feet.

"Jason, please." Was it possible to act normal when the future was shaping up so precariously?

"None of your *please*," he threw over his shoulder. "All you're good for is opening old wounds."

"I don't want you to go." She, too, had no difficulty negotiating the stairs at a run. "Tali and I will be alone."

"You're surely not nervous?" He spun about, finding her much closer than he expected. Her dark hair flew around her pale perfect face. Her eyes glittered like gems. Her mouth, her beautiful mouth with its full bottom lip was the only colour about her. Rose red. Her dress was an exquisite ice-white, fantastically pretty, one shouldered, the soft chiffon scattered all over with little silver beads and shimmery things that caught the light. "I pity the man who tried to get the better of you!" he grated.

"*You* did!" she answered with intensity. "I've never truly been free of you."

"So why do you want me to stay?" He retraced his steps, standing over her, staring down into her troubled face.

"Because…because…" Her eyes started to fill with tears, rapidly increasing his already sizzling desire.

"Say it," he ordered. "You understand, Liv. I want you to say it. Now!"

She knew he wouldn't tolerate any further provocation. "Because I ache for you," she said, her voice trembling. "You, Jason. No-one else."

"You'll let me sleep with you?" The words came out more harshly than he intended, but couldn't she see what she was doing to him?

Colour bloomed in her cheeks. "If you think Tali will sleep soundly."

"And I have to get up at four o'clock in the morning to go home?" He smiled slightly but his expression remained taut. "I'm a very busy man after all."

In an instant she was vibrating with anger, interpreting the tautness as insolence. "Then do what you want," she said sharply, thinking he was trying to humiliate her. "Feel free to go. I'll lock up after you."

"Will you just!" He raised a sardonic brow. "You've just issued me with an invitation, Olivia. I'm going to take it. We're both past games."

What was she supposed to do? Olivia stalked to the door, the rigidity of her body language indicating he should leave. "I don't like your attitude, Jason," she said. "Tali and I will be quite safe. You can't have forgotten we have an excellent security system."

"Not to mention your eyes looking daggers, those sharp little teeth which you've already used on me, and your long nails. I might have to carry you up those stairs screaming and kicking but I will do it," he promised.

"Would you really like to hear me scream?"

"Possibly." His mouth twisted. "Little screams in my ear when I'm making love to you."

The shift to tender eroticism quite vanquished her.

He wasted no time. He moved to take her quiescent body

into his arms, one long arm reaching out to switch off all
the exterior lights and the huge, multibranched chandelier
that blazed over their heads.

''You're an aggravating woman,'' he said, staring down
into her face.

''I am.''

His arms settled on either side of her while he shut then
locked the front door. ''We're quite alone.'' His eyes burned
over her.

''Yes, I know.''

''Except for Tali who's sleeping the deep sleep only children are capable of.''

She reached out to him, slipping several buttons of his
blue shirt, then she slid her hand in over his bare chest,
splaying her fingers through the tangle of hair. ''Don't you
want to know who my last lover was?''

''No.'' He bent forward to kiss her, a brief taste of what
was to come, yet she almost whimpered at the rush of pleasure. ''Whoever it was your heart wasn't in it.''

''That goes for them all,'' she said, when they were few.
''I could never block *you* out.''

''And who *were* they?'' he whispered against her throat,
his mouth moving to kiss the shoulder laid bare by her dress;
his hand to the chiffon folds over her breast, the sensitive
tips of her nipples flaring at the touch of his thumb.

She couldn't have moved even if she'd wanted to. Her
body betrayed her anyway. Pleasure held her like a velvet
trap.

''You can't escape me, Liv.'' His voice was quiet but
vibrating with a lover's emotion.

''I don't want to.'' With one hand she grasped the front
of his shirt, pulling him ever closer to her, the other hand
at the back of his neck.

The look in his eyes, the blue of sapphires, the blue of

the ocean, had the hot blood glittering in her arteries. "You're *my* girl. You always were. Always will be."

He lifted her effortlessly, her long hair falling free as he strode up the graceful flight of stairs, to the moonlight and roses of her beautiful bedroom.

CHAPTER TEN

THERE was no sleep. They made love into the predawn as though they had to make up for the lost years. Their passion for each other was for once unguarded. There was no place for conflict, for control, for the self-disciplines they had imposed on themselves. There was no place either for alienation or restraint. It was an extraordinary night, a long waited exploration when time no longer mattered...

Jason was an infinitely skilled lover. Her body welcomed him as it had never welcomed another. He aroused in her sensations so exquisite they broke her heart; sensations of such intensity they drew her out of the deep void in which she had buried herself, tumbling her fathoms into a glittering sea of love where her body was weightless and incredibly she could breathe.

She was rising...reaching for him; Jason easing into her body, the tumultuous penetration; the throbbing, rhythmical, sensuality too wonderful to describe. Trembling moments poised on the brink before the blind rush to climax; the desperate desire, the convulsive rapture. The starburst! A brilliant display behind tightly locked lids. The reverie of endless contractions, vibrations that resounded deep within the body.

The most exquisite indolence! Satiated, they rested naked in each other's arms until inevitably such was their hunger they slipped back into that ravishing eroticism where the only sounds were broken endearments, laboured breaths, little gasps and long drawn out rapturous moans. There was nothing they would not give to each other.

"You've exhausted me," he laughed. "You're so demanding.'' He turned on his side to drop the sweetest kiss on her open mouth.

"You can't go on?" she teased.

"We'll see."

Afterwards they showered together, soaping each other extravagantly, all laughter stopping abruptly as passion overtook them. Desire was more intoxicating than any drug. Only in the cool of dawn when Jason left quietly did Olivia fall into an exhausted sleep, waking abruptly at seven because she had Tali on her mind. She threw back the sheet that was her only covering, pulling her satin robe around her and belting it tightly before she walked down the hallway to check on Tali.

The little girl was all curled up, sleeping deeply. Probably she'd sleep another hour or so after her broken night. Jason had a few things to check on but he'd promised to come back around midday when all three of them could have lunch together, perhaps a picnic, Tali would love that. There was plenty of food left over. Olivia resisted the urge to go back to bed. She was still in a state of euphoria thinking all these years later she had finally found herself in Jason. She returned to her room to dress then she went downstairs to the kitchen to brew herself a fragrant cup of coffee. Her mood was so buoyant she felt she had somehow captured some of the stars that had exploded behind her closed eyes.

When Jason arrived at the house he saw the porch light was on. He was absolutely certain he had turned it off. Break-ins were few and far between in the area. Many people continued to leave their homes with the back doors unlocked. He didn't go as far as that but he'd never felt anxious about leaving the cottage unattended.

It took him a few moments to park the four-wheel drive then he was up on the verandah fitting the key to the lock of the front door. Before he even entered the house he felt sure someone had been there. Possibly they were still there. He felt no fear. Unless some lunatic was going to confront him at gun-point he knew how to handle himself.

"Anyone there?" he called in a loud commanding voice. "You'd better come out because I'll damned well find you." Perhaps it was kids? Surely not.

He paused to pick up a small cast iron frying pan from the kitchen hoping he didn't have to use it.

"Come out," he thundered. Hell it could be anybody— a vagrant passing through.

A figure stood in the hallway. A woman with extremely short bleached blond hair and small pinched features. She was wearing one his T-shirts, her legs bare, her hair standing away from her head in brittle spikes, her small face showing evidence of the kind of life she'd been living.

"Hello, Jason," she said.

"Megan!" he exclaimed. She looked very different. One tough little chick.

"Are you going to brain me with that?" A provocative smile crossed her small face.

"What are you doing here, Megan?" He turned back to place the frying pan on the kitchen counter. "How did you get in?"

Megan rolled her eyes in feigned surprise. "Shit, Jason," she said coarsely, "I know how to pick a lock, but I didn't have to—a back window was ajar. I found a box in the shed…it was dead easy to climb in. I dossed down in Natalie's bed. I'm sure the little darling won't mind. Was it you that made the bedroom so pretty and comfy? Bet it was. Still the doting dad."

"I asked you what you're doing here," he said.

"And where were you last night?" she countered, unabashed. She'd had her fair share of smacks in the face but she knew belting women around wasn't Jason's style. "Leave the kid with the old girl while you had it off with your precious Olivia?" She put real venom into that. "Oh yes, I know she's back. I know Linfield died. I know you're working at Havilah. Sounds like you've got it made.''

''All of which is absolutely no business of yours,'' Jason said coldly. ''We're divorced remember?''

''Natalie is still my kid.''

Jason's eyes flashed. ''You didn't want her. You couldn't wait to be rid of her. As they say a cat would make a better mother.''

Megan padded into the living room and curled into an armchair, her posture suggesting she was trying to be seductive. ''How do you know I haven't changed?'' she challenged, allowing the neck of his T-shirt to fall off one shoulder. ''How do you know I'm not thinking of remarrying? I might want my kid back.''

His mouth twisted in disgust. ''You're talking to the wrong guy, Megan. Far from remarrying you look like you've been living rough. What is this, a bid for money? I don't have money, Megan.''

''Your precious Olivia does.'' Again the jealousy and venom spilled out. ''Harry Linfield was worth millions and millions.''

''All of which is tied up.'' Jason had no trouble telling the lie. ''Not that that's relevant. You're the last person in the world Olivia would give money to, if you've decided on a spot of blackmail. Olivia wouldn't give money to me, either. All these years later she still feels I betrayed her.''

''You did, though, didn't you, Jason sweetie?''

It was said with a good deal of bravado, but Jason fancied he heard a note ring false. ''I'm pretty damned slow but I guess that could be a lie as well?'' He stared at her, waiting for her response.

''It's the truth, pal,'' she retorted swiftly, sitting up straight. ''I was a virgin, don't you forget it, Natalie is your kid.''

He continued to study her with brilliant assessing eyes. ''I think I'd kill you if you were lying to me, Megan.''

"I'm not lying to you, sweetie." She fell into her raunchy pose again. "Tali's your kid. You look great by the way, sexier than ever!"

"You're not," he said coolly. "So you're wasting your time with all that flashing."

"Too bad!" She shrugged. "A lot of the time it works. Anyway, I don't want to take the kid off you. I'm sure we can work something out."

"Like what?" It was shocking but conclusive DNA match-ups sprang into his mind, even as he struggled to reject the smallest possibility Tali wasn't his.

"I want to see her again, mind you." Megan tried to assume a motherly demeanour, but her eyes were cold. "Sweet little thing! I suppose she's grown into a holy terror. She was heading that way. I never heard a kid give more cheek!"

"I call it spirit," Jason corrected with quiet contempt. "She was trying to defend herself against a bitch of a mother."

"Oh dear!" Megan attempted a jibe.

"Have you no love in your heart for her?" Jason asked. "Has life taught you nothing?"

"It's taught me I'm on my own." Megan nodded her head with so much vehemence it bounced. "The big love of my life is me. I've had a tough time. Men are such bastards. Strangely enough that doesn't include you, Jason, honey. I have to say it, you're a real gentleman. I think I still love ya. How is that possible?"

"You don't love me, Megan. You don't even know me. If you're in trouble I can give you a little money, that's all. You can't stay here. You can't upset Tali. I won't have that."

"I'm her mother nonetheless," Megan said pointedly. "I'm not done with her or you at all! The thing is I have a yen to be respectable, Jason. The last guy I was with treated me like a slut. I'm done with that. I'm thinking maybe a quarter of a million bucks?''

Jason's laugh was harsh. ''You want a quarter of a million to be gone? And when that runs out? What then?''

Megan swung her legs to the floor. ''I promise you I won't ask for more, Jason,'' she said earnestly. ''I thought I might get myself a job on the Gold Coast, maybe at the casino. I'm good at handling money. The Gold Coast is pretty ritzy. I might find myself a rich good-looking guy.''

''Then you'd better let your hair go back to its original colour and put on some weight,'' Jason advised. ''You don't look good, Megan. I'm not trying to be cruel. I'm telling you, you have to start looking after yourself. You have to stop putting yourself in dangerous situations. Do you ever contact your parents?''

''Hell, why would I want to do that?'' Megan exclaimed, running a defensive hand through her spiky hair. ''They don't give a damn about me. They never did. Maybe Mum did a bit but she was powerless beside Dad. How I hate him. And Sean.''

''I'm sorry, Megan,'' Jason said. ''I wish your home-life could have been better for you but you have to take responsibility for your own actions. You had a daughter. You had a husband who stood by you.'' I don't know for how long, Jason thought but didn't say.

Megan waved a dismissive hand. ''I know you tried, Jason, but you couldn't love me.'' She pressed the balls of her palms to her eyes. ''Why couldn't you love me?''

''Megan, I hardly knew you. We weren't at all close. I loved Olivia. I've always loved Olivia.''

''Olivia! I'm sick of hearing about her,'' Megan said wearily. ''Wouldn't you think she'd have found someone else by now?''

''How do you know she hasn't?'' Jason asked tonelessly, unwilling to expose Olivia.

''Because she bloody well loves you,'' Megan said.

''Did you hate Olivia?'' Jason asked.

''What do you think?'' Megan sneered. ''Everyone loved Olivia. No-one loved me.''

''So what did you do?'' Jason moved closer, standing over her.

''What do you mean?'' Megan pulled back in her arm-chair.

''Did you plan what happened that night? That night I can never remember.''

''Don't be daft!'' she snorted. ''You made love to me, Jason. You were so beautiful. That body! Then when you were done you slept like a log.''

''More like a coma.''

He was looking at her oddly. ''I didn't plan anything, Jason.'' Megan allowed her voice to crack. ''It just happened. Now I want a life and you have to help me. Because if you don't,'' she paused to threaten him, ''I swear I'll take Natalie off you and break your heart.''

When the phone rang Olivia was almost afraid to answer it, afraid it might be Carlo De Luca at the other end, that he might want to speak to her. After the wonderment of last night, the putting aside of all her anxieties, they came crashing back. She picked up the receiver, said hello, and just as she feared, Carlo De Luca's attractive voice answered with some intensity. ''Olivia, I must speak to you. Leanne will be ringing later to thank you for last night, but that's not what we need to talk about. I know it's hard. You're the innocent party in all this but you *know*, don't you?''

The accusation was unmistakable. It hung heavily on the line. She did indeed *know*. Momentarily Olivia squeezed her eyes tight. ''Help me, Carlo. What are we talking about?'' she decided to stall.

''We're talking about Natalie, Olivia,'' he answered bluntly. ''She's the living image of my sister Gina at the same age. You know what that means, don't you? She's *mine*."

For what seemed like an interminable time Olivia couldn't find words.

"What do you want me to say, Carlo?" she asked finally. "I saw a resemblance of course. More to you than Gina—I haven't seen Gina in years. I was just dumbfounded."

"*You* were dumbfounded?" Carlo interjected, his voice rising. "What do you think *I* was?"

"Carlo, I'm sorry," she said. "Sorry, sorry, sorry. Sorry for us all. You must realize Jason believes Tali to be his. He loves her. I think if you took her off him it would kill him."

"Olivia, she's *mine*. You understand what that means, don't you? She's my flesh and blood. My mum and dad are her grandparents. Gina's her aunt. Have you any idea how my mother would react if she laid eyes on Natalie? She'd be devastated then terribly, terribly angry. Not with you or Jason but Megan! That miserable lying little bitch."

Olivia looked around her hurriedly to be sure Tali was still upstairs watching her video.

"Why did she do it?" Carlo groaned.

"She mightn't have known," Olivia suggested unhappily, lowering her voice a notch.

"Olivia, you can't believe that!" Carlo responded, disgusted. "Okay Megan and I had sex. Only once in the back of my car. Never again. But I can assure you of this. She was no vulnerable little chick randy old me picked up, much less a virgin. She knew exactly what she was doing."

"She couldn't have, Carlo," Olivia found herself defending Megan. "She got pregnant."

Carlo sounded utterly exasperated. "Listen, she told me she was on the pill. I had condoms anyhow. I remember particularly, because she also told me she was never going to be stuck with a kid. She was adamant about that as though kids would never be on her agenda. Obviously something went wrong—I bet if she thought about it she'd have identified the cause. She must have forgotten to take the pills religiously or she had a fairly severe stomach bug and the pill went straight through her.''

''What is it you expect me to do, Carlo?'' Olivia asked, her mind grappling with these new implications.

Carlo didn't hesitate. ''We all have to meet,'' he said. ''I've seen my daughter, Olivia. It was meant to be, I truly believe that. Now there's no turning back.''

''So what are you saying?'' Olivia asked, afraid of what all this would do to her life. ''You expect me to organise a meeting here?''

''There, anywhere. It can't be here. My parents would be shocked out of their minds. I have to break it to them and to Leanne fairly gently.''

''And what of Leanne?'' Olivia couldn't control the fact her voice came out sharply. ''How do you think she'll react to a ready-made step-daughter?''

There was a short pause on the line. ''She mightn't be all that happy,'' Carlo ventured slowly. ''But no-one, even Leanne, is going to stop me. As it happens Lee thought Natalie was adorable.''

''She thought Tali was Jason's you mean,'' Olivia retorted with considerable irony. ''Jason thinks Tali is Jason's. What about Jason, Carlo? Try to remember him. Jason has taken wonderful care of Tali for nearly seven years. Now he's supposed to let her walk out of his life? What about Tali? Have you really thought it through? She loves her daddy.''

''*I'm* her daddy, Olivia,'' Carlo replied as though that was all that needed to be said as perhaps it was. ''I'm thinking of all the things you're talking about. Don't you think I've considered the massive upsets? But I told you. I'm not turning back. Natalie is my child. Child of my body. She'd be instantly recognisable to my family. We're all caring adults here. We have to work on this. We have to make the transition as painless as possible. I'm not suggesting for a minute we'd ride rough shod over Jason and his feelings. For such a smart guy I can't believe how he let Megan put it over him.''

''Are you saying she did it deliberately?'' Olivia asked, absolutely appalled.

''Of course she did,'' Carlo said with conviction. ''You had to know Megan had a crush on Jason. Hell, they all did. All the girls. But he never looked at anyone but you.''

''He must have slept with Megan at least once,'' Olivia said weakly.

Carlo's oath was low and violent. ''If I hadn't gone away to study I'd have been able to have a word with Jason. I'd have told him Megan Duffy was a lying, manipulative little so and so. My guess is she not only tricked him into marrying her, he mightn't have had sex with her at all. The gossip was he was drunk but I never saw Jason Corey drunk. He'd always have a few drinks with us guys but he'd never go overboard. Remember how Jason was everyone's hero? He's a genuinely great guy. He never made a damned fool of himself like me. My guess is someone got to take care of him. He was at Sean Duffy's birthday party, wasn't he? Hell, how did the two of you get mixed up with that family? It could have been Megan, I wouldn't put it past her.''

Olivia shook her head in sick disbelief. ''If what you're saying is true, Megan did a terrible thing. She denied you the truth. She lied to Jason. She shattered Jason's and my plans. Would you have married her, Carlo?''

Carlo answered truthfully. ''No. Probably both of us would have been better off. But she'd have had my support, my family's support, we'd have found a way. My mother would never abandon her grandchild. Or me, no matter what I did. That's why I'm saying now, we have to find a way to make this work.''

''And what of Megan? You really don't see her as a complication? I've had bad vibes about Megan. What if she turns up again? What if she sees some angle she can work? She's indisputably Tali's mother. Even allowing for the extraordinary resemblance and your gut feeling I would assume DNA samples would be needed to conclusively prove paternity?''

''Of course,'' Carlo responded, his tone clinical. ''But I know they're not needed. If you need time to speak to Jason—seeing you together last night there's no doubting you still love and need each other—maybe we can organise a meeting tomorrow some time. But this must be decided before Leanne and I go back to Brisbane. Can I leave it with you, Olivia?'' he asked, a deep plea in his voice. ''You've had a rough deal, but as fate would have it, you're the one caught in the middle.''

It was almost lunchtime before Jason returned. Olivia moving out onto the front terrace to greet him was immediately struck by his pallor. He was white beneath the deep tan.

Olivia took a deep breath until she thought her lungs might burst. ''What is it? Is everything okay?'' She grabbed for his hand, held it, staring up into his face. ''Jason, what is it?'' Inexplicably she felt like she was being taken back in time to the day when he told her he couldn't marry her.

''I've got some bad news, Liv,'' he said. ''Megan's back.''

Despite her fears Olivia felt such shock for a moment she couldn't speak. ''Of course she's back!'' Finally she exploded. ''She'll never go away. She wants to spoil things for us forever! What does she want?'' she demanded.

''What do you think?'' Jason gave a hollow laugh that vibrated in his chest. ''Money.''

Olivia's silver eyes flashed. ''You mean if we give her money she'll leave us alone?''

''So she said.''

''And who could believe her? She's lied and lied and lied.

We'd give her money and she'd only come back. I don't like the idea of being blackmailed.''

"She's not blackmailing you, Liv. She's blackmailing me.''

"Where is she?'' Olivia felt her nostrils flare with anger.

Jason turned his head. "She's in the car, with instructions to stay there.''

"She has the hide to show herself here on Havilah? To me? I'll be having a word with your ex-wife, Jason,'' Olivia told him furiously. "How could you bring her here?''

"She's demanding to see Tali,'' Jason said, a hard tone to his voice.

"And you said she *could?*''

Jason bristled. "She can do an awful lot of harm, Liv. She *is* Tali's mother and she's saying she wants her back. The courts treat mothers better than they do fathers—I don't believe I'm in a position to refuse her. I don't want to upset you any more than you are already. I'm very uncomfortable with the whole situation but I'll see what Tali has to say about this. If she wants to see her mother I'll take them both back to my place.''

Olivia felt her anger swelling again. "Last night, Jason, you told me you loved me, that you'd never stopped loving me, that you wanted us to be together for always, that *this* time we'd actually go through with a marriage. Now you're telling me that Megan Duffy, the cause of so much heartache is here in the estate car?''

"What did you want me to do, run over her?'' Jason asked in a kind of anguish. "She's Tali's *mother,* Liv. A pretty terrible mother but a mother all the same and she's a damned good actress. She could get it together to convince the Family Court she should at least share custody.''

"But she'll go away if we give her money?'' Olivia was trying very hard to stay in control. "How much?''

Jason's jaw tightened. "A quarter of a million.''

Olivia laughed. "Now there's a measly amount for little

Megan Duffy to ask for! Why didn't she go for a full million?"

"You're used to money, Liv," Jason pointed out. "A quarter of a million would be a great fortune to Megan. Then again I haven't got a million I could part with."

"No, but I have." Olivia felt exceedingly angry. "She knows that. She knows we're back together. She knows Harry was a rich man. She knows I've inherited. Was she waiting for you when you got home?"

Jason sighed deeply. "She was."

"In your *home!* I'm surprised she wasn't in your bed."

"Give it a rest, Liv," Jason warned.

Olivia didn't seem to catch the warning. "This is my worst nightmare come to life!" she fumed. "I can't stand here talking about this. I'm going to have a word with Megan Duffy. You go find Tali. She's out on the loggia working on a jigsaw puzzle—she wanted to have it done before you arrived."

"What are you going to say, Liv?" Jason looked anxious.

"Leave that to me."

The crisp, decisive note in her voice reminded Jason of Harry.

"This is one confrontation that's been a long time coming."

Jason had parked the four-wheel drive in the shade of the poincianas in full, glorious bloom. Waves of spent blossom were lying on the grass and on the hood of the car. "Get out, Megan," Olivia said, using the sort of voice she reserved for the most rebellious student. "We're going for a little walk."

Megan got out. She was wearing a short sundress, yellow with sprigs of orange flowers, no makeup, her hair bleached yellow and gelled into a style that didn't flatter her small, thin features, yellow thongs on her feet. "So how's it going, princess?'' she asked insolently, showing a side of herself Olivia had never seen.

Olivia contemplated her out of eyes that were cool, almost pitying. ''Once upon a time I thought I liked you, Megan. No one else liked you, which should have given me pause, but no, I tried to help you. I thought you'd had an unhappy home life and you could do with a friend. I even asked you to be my bridesmaid. Of course you were a lot prettier then, Megan. What have you done to yourself in the meantime? You obviously haven't been eating and that porcupine hairstyle doesn't suit you.''

Megan looked up at the taller Olivia and glared. ''So okay I'm going to change it—we all can't look like you. I'm here to see my daughter. Any objections?''

''Miss her, do you?'' Olivia asked pleasantly.

''I'm not a complete bitch,'' Megan replied.

''Oh, yes, you are,'' Olivia assured her in a composed voice. ''I'm amazed you can't see it. For one thing you're a pathological liar. Do you know what *that* means?''

''I don't have to put up with this.'' Megan tried a sneer that didn't quite come off.

''You do, Megan. You really do. You made the mistake of coming onto my land. This is a very serious matter, the consequences of which you'll be lucky to escape. Tali isn't Jason's child.''

Immediately Megan lost what colour she had. ''She bloody well is!'' she protested, holding her flat stomach as though she'd been stabbed.

''She bloody well *isn't*,'' Olivia corrected gently. ''Tali is Carlo De Luca's child as you very well know.''

Megan visibly recoiled. ''Prove it.''

''Very easily, Megan.'' Olivia continued along the path shaded by the interlocking branches of the poincianas. ''You're not getting this, are you? Nearly everyone I would have thought has heard of DNA. It's the carrier of genetic information, it will tell us exactly who Tali's father is.

That's if we want conclusive proof. Actually she's the very image of Carlo's younger sister, Gina, at the same age. Extraordinary how blood will out! I pity you, Megan, I really do. Wait until Mrs. De Luca comes after you. Good grief, you'll probably need hospitalising. You lied and lied didn't you, Megan? I only hope everyone is going to understand. I mean I have every right to pull your hair out but I'm not going to do it. So distasteful. I bet Jason didn't have sex with you at all?"

"He bloody *did*." Megan's voice was filled with real shock.

"No, Megan." Olivia shook her head. "I think not. Your lying days are over. You blinded me with your quiet demeanour—I didn't see you for what you really are. You wanted to spite me and you wanted Jason full stop. You saw an opportunity so you moved in. Far from being drunk, Jason was probably drugged. It could have been you who spiked his drink with your dirty little hands."

"Shut up. Shut up. All right." Megan stared back defiantly. "*I* didn't do it."

"So it was Sean or one of his deplorable friends?" Olivia continued conversationally. "But you saw your chance, Megan. Here was Jason about to stumble into your waiting arms. Another woman's fiancé, but what the hell! All's fair in love and war. It was handy your aunt was out of town. You managed to get Jason to her place, didn't you? I daresay you snuggled up to him naked in bed. That would have been a real turn-on. Everything about you is odious. The one thing I'm sure of—God forgive me for ever doubting him—Jason didn't make love to you. He would have been incapable. Not because he was drunk or drugged but because he was faithful to me. We were to be married.

"When you found out you were pregnant you knew what to do. Trick that knight in shining armour, Jason Corey, into marrying you. It was the opportunity of a lifetime. It would never come again and there had to be a child otherwise you'd have had an abortion. Never mind about poor silly Olivia—she'd fly into a rage, women do. She wouldn't stop and say, Hang on! We need proof. She decided the man she loved was guilty right off. I blame myself for that, Megan.''

''And so you should!'' Megan gave a bitter, narrow smile. ''If you wanted to be a high-minded fool who was I to stand in your way? I didn't care about you. You've never had to put up with the things I've had to. I reckon Jason is the only person I've ever loved—he doesn't have a mean bone in his body. So I didn't sleep with him before we got married? I slept with him plenty after. He was *my* husband, you know, Olivia dear, not yours. What we didn't get up to on our honeymoon!'' She rolled expressive eyes. ''I've never had a better lover.''

Olivia stood completely still, though she wanted to smack the smirk off Megan's face. ''You must have felt such triumph? For how long? The whole five minutes it took for the wedding ceremony? I bet Jason couldn't get through a day without thinking of me. It must have been really, *really* awful finding out he could never care for you.''

Megan flushed darkly and stepped back. ''Yeah, well, you didn't have him, either. At least I made sure of that.'' Megan threw a nervous glance ahead. Olivia had led her under a pergola of stone pillars festooned with a dazzling gold trumpet vine that had been allowed to overgrow to such an extent it formed a dense tunnel. Megan had the dismal notion there mightn't be light at the other end. Olivia wasn't the tender hearted push-over she'd once been—she looked steely. ''So how far are we going to walk?''

''For as long as it takes,'' Olivia answered calmly, breaking off a spray of blossoms. ''You're going to go away, Megan. You're never going to come back. You're going to get yourself a nice respectable job some place. Try Tasmania, that should be far enough.''

Megan's laugh was hollow. ''You think that's going to happen do you? Never mind you finally figured it out. Jason to this very day, *hasn't*. It's really pathetic, but he loves that kid. He thinks she's his. You haven't told him your little secret, have you, Olivia? You love him. You don't want him to suffer. You can live with the fact Tali isn't his every single minute of the day, but you won't tell Jason. He thinks the world of that kid. It would kill him to know she isn't his. All I'm asking is a little nest egg to set me up. I'm not a rich bitch like you. I didn't have any doting old fool of an uncle to leave me a fortune. We can work this out, Olivia. You're smart. You'll do it for Jason.''

"And for Tali," Olivia said. "Oh, I forgot, you're not interested in your little daughter."

"What a ridiculous nickname," Megan snorted, feeling strangely disoriented within this dense tunnel of pungent flowers and the shifting light as the tumbling branches of the climber moved. "She's Natalie," she insisted. "After a movie star I kinda liked. Okay, so you're fond of Natalie, all the better.''

Olivia continued her unhurried stroll although she was aware of Megan's strange discomfort. "What about Carlo De Luca?" she asked. "You don't think he has the right to know he fathered a child?"

Megan's fair skin blotched red. "Forget about Carlo. What he doesn't know won't hurt him. He's in Sydney anyway.''

"Brisbane. He transferred to Brisbane."

They emerged from the gold and green grotto at long last. Now Megan literally dug in her toes. "That was like swimming underwater," she complained. "Few gardens are as big as this. There are too many areas." She was averse to walking through the arched entrance to the walled garden. It looked like it had come from the ruins of some temple. "Brisbane is still a thousand miles away," she pointed out, shrugging her thin shoulders. "Big country!"

"Small world. What about his parents, his sister? What

happens when they lay eyes on Tali. They'll see the blood tie straight away.''

''So *you* say.'' Megan cut her short. ''I used to wonder when the penny would drop with Jason but it never did. Listen I don't want to go any further, it's too bloody spooky. I don't like all these arches and statues and things, those old stone urns on stands. I like everything new, modern. I like to be able to see where I'm going, too. I don't like your ponds and all those white lilies—you could drown in them ponds.''

''Nonsense,'' Olivia said bracingly. ''Havilah's gardens are famous in this part of the world, Megan. Obviously you're not a nature lover. As for the lakes! Water views and pavilions are essential in a hot humid climate. I think you're nervous because you have such a guilty conscience. All this beauty defeats you. No need to be nervous of me, though. I won't drown you.''

''I bet you'd like to.'' Megan shuddered, far more comfortable out in the full sun.

''Believe me, Megan, I don't want to lay a hand on you,'' Olivia told her in complete honesty. ''I can't speak for the De Luca's of course. They're very volatile and they *will* see the resemblance.''

''Oh, all this perfume! It's enough to make you drunk!'' Megan burst out, for the first time sounding nervous and overwrought. Her nostrils were assailed by a thousand languorous fragrances which for some reason made her feel almost hysterical. ''People only see what they want to see. There's Jason, a really smart guy in so many other ways, who thinks Tali has his eyes.'' Megan hit her fingers against her forehead. ''They're Carlo's eyes.''

''Of course they are!'' Olivia agreed. ''They're Gina De Luca's eyes as well and now I think about it Salvatore's, Carlo's father. Blue eyes are so striking in a Mediterranean face.''

''No reason why they should see her.'' Megan lost all her bravado. ''Change her appearance a bit. You could do it.''

''Plastic surgery, contact lenses?'' Olivia enquired with quiet sarcasm, stopping beside an elegant garden seat. ''The truth will out, Megan.''

Megan nibbled hard on her lip while she considered. ''Make it a hundred thousand,'' she said. ''That should take care of it. I promise you I won't bother you again.''

''Why don't you tell that to Carlo De Luca?'' Olivia suggested.

''What do you mean?'' Megan lifted her narrow head, fear in her eyes.

''I mean, Megan, Carlo De Luca knows. He's staying with his parents over Christmas and last night he came here for dinner. As it happened Tali was fast asleep upstairs. Incredibly she woke just as Carlo was leaving—a bad dream—she rushed downstairs to find Jason, found her *real* father instead. Carlo recognised her at once. It was quite extraordinary. A revelation.''

''No!'' A shudder tore through Megan's slight frame. She clutched at the garden seat for support. ''What did he say?''

''He said—'' Olivia looked back at Megan ever so pityingly ''—wait until Mama finds out.'' She's a very formidable woman, Bella De Luca. I wouldn't want to be the person to upset her. She'll be very upset with you, Megan. She might be tempted to take a kitchen knife to you.''

Megan choked. ''Are you crazy! I won't see her.''

''Or Carlo?''

''No way! I don't want any trouble. I've had a rotten life. You don't know the half of it.''

''I suppose not,'' Olivia said, unable despite everything to put pity aside. ''You've been the cause of a lot of suffering, Megan. Are you fully aware of that?''

''Ah, get out! You're as happy as a pig in a poke,'' Megan rallied, straightening up. ''You've got Jason back haven't you?'' she asked cheekily. ''You've got this bloody great place. It's like your own private kingdom.'' She waved her arms about. ''What have *I* got?''

''Probably what you deserve, Megan.'' Olivia started to move on. ''Let me ask you. Do you really want to see Tali? I certainly won't prevent you, I'm no heartless monster.''

''No, you're a bloody saint!'' Megan jeered. ''Remember saints are really the worst at spotting sinners. I played you and Jason for mugs. Never mind with your kind little gestures, Olivia, I don't want to see Natalie. I wouldn't know what to say to her. I've got no feeling for her anyway.''

''That's very difficult to accept!'' Olivia sighed deeply. ''I suppose one might be able to trace your inability to love your child back to things that went on in your own childhood. Either way, you're the loser, Megan. Tali's a delightful little girl. She's really intelligent. Pretty. Funny. I'll tell you something else. *Carlo wants her!*''

Megan's delicate jaw dropped. Clearly she hadn't expected to hear that. ''He doesn't. He couldn't.'' She shook her head.

''Not everyone's like you, Megan. The bond between parent and child is the most powerful bond there is. Carlo wants his daughter.''

Megan looked like her whole world was about to implode on her. ''So what about Jason?'' she croaked, her small features looking more pinched than ever.

''Ah, yes, Jason your trump card! The reality is you have no bargaining power, Megan. Jason doesn't know yet but sadly he will. Now, I tell you what I'm going to do. It will be my very last kindness to you, one I'm sure you won't refuse. I'm going to write you a cheque for $10,000 which is something you truly don't deserve. But you are Tali's mother and I still feel some pity for you. Perhaps if you'd had a different life you wouldn't be what you are now.

''What you have to do to get it, is take a train or a plane or a bus out of here. Today, not tomorrow, today. I might change my mind otherwise. Ten thousand dollars should set you up until you get a job. You can look the part when you want to. The waif hairdo will suit you if you forget the hot spikes and go back to your natural colour. In return, you won't breathe a word to Jason about Carlo being Tali's true father. Certainly not when he drives you to the train or the airport. I'll give you cash to cover your ticket to Brisbane. You can work out your final destination from there. If you say anything I'll know from Jason's reactions and cancel the cheque. I don't know why I'm saying this, Megan, but I wish you well. Just don't ever come back.''

Olivia left Megan standing beside the car while she walked back across the lawn to the homestead.

Jason was sitting in a white wicker armchair, his long legs stretched out in front of him, seemingly staring into space.

''Where's Tali?'' Olivia asked in surprise, looking around for the little girl.

''She's hiding upstairs,'' Jason said laconically, rising slowly to his impressive height. ''It's a truly appalling state of affairs, but Tali doesn't want to see her mother. I'm not going to be the one to force her.''

''Who's suggesting you do?'' Olivia had the notion his brilliant blue eyes were a shade hostile.

''You never know with you, Liv.'' Jason shook his head. ''Megan could have dumped a sob story on you. It took me a heck of a time to get over the fact you asked her to be a bridesmaid but I went along with it—brides privilege and all that. I truly don't like to say this, but Megan is poison.''

Olivia gave way to a flare of temper. ''*You* brought her here, I didn't issue any invitation. Please don't take it out on me, Jason. I know you're upset.''

''Who the hell else have I got to take it out on?'' he responded, his mouth wry.'' Tali has been the only good thing in life since you left me. Now Megan, complete with a punk hairdo and skinny little legs, is back to blackmail me. I can't let Tali go—I have to look after her. I know Megan. She'd do anything to spite us. Hell, she'd sell Tali if she could get away with it.''

''Megan's not going to do anything,'' Olivia said, looking back across at him. ''I left her standing beside the car. She doesn't want to see Tali, by the way. Are you sure she actually gave birth or was it a phantom pregnancy?''

''You know it's not mandatory for mothers to love their babies, Liv,'' Jason said. ''Mothers have done unspeakable things to their children. Probably it has something to do with their own past experiences. Megan wasn't fitted for the role of mother—she has no capacity. She saw Tali almost as the enemy from day one. They just didn't click, hard as that is to comprehend. Thankfully it's not the general picture. I bet she tried to blackmail you as well?''

Olivia replied with a groan. ''Not that I was seriously considering a quarter of a million. I'm not completely insane.''

''No, but you're pretty damned softhearted,'' Jason retorted. ''Except with me.''

''You don't mean that?'' Olivia was trying to recall only hours before they were making perfect love.

''You never wanted to see me again, remember?'' Jason spun about. ''Oh, hell, I'm sorry I said that, forget it. Megan has upset me good and proper.''

And there was plenty more upset to come. ''Well I've sorted her out,'' Olivia told him in a more gentle tone of voice. ''I've managed to beat her back from $250,000 to $10,000 providing she leaves right away.''

''And she went for it?'' Jason turned to stare at her.

''I didn't get a peep out of her!'' Olivia raised her brows. ''I suppose at some point in life we all start to get smart.''

Jason threw back his head and laughed. ''How do we know she won't come at this again when the $10,000 runs out?''

"I might have told her I'd employ a hit-man," Olivia said with black humour.

"Liv, darling, she's probably trying to milk this for all it's worth."

"I don't think so." Olivia shook her head. "Now I'm going into the house to write the cheque. I'll also give her some cash so she can take a bus, a train, a plane or the pillion seat of a motor bike out, as far as Brisbane, that is. If you wouldn't mind, Jason—as she is your ex-wife—I'd like you to drive her off Havilah to whatever terminal she wants to go."

He let his eyes rest on her for the longest time. "No need to overplay the grand lady, Liv, your appearance says it all. Naturally I'll reimburse you for whatever it is you give her. I don't run around with a cheque book in my pocket."

"Thank you, Jason," Olivia said. "Being so damned decent is one of the things I like most about you. However, permit this over-the-top lady to say the payout I effected is a damned sight less than what she was first talking about."

"Good work!" Jason sketched a brief salute.

Olivia moved swiftly towards the entrance hall. At the door she paused. "By the way, while I'm inside I'll find Tali and tell her she's free to do exactly as she pleases."

"Take all the time you like," Jason said.

The picnic lunch didn't happen. Jason drove Megan away. Tali came to stand beside Olivia as she watched from behind the drawing room's curtains.

"Has she gone?" Tali shuddered, clutching Olivia's hand tightly.

"Why couldn't you see your mummy, sweetheart?" Olivia asked, thinking she would have given anything to have had her mother live. "Is it because she hit you?"

"I thought she was going to *kill* me, you mean," Tali said with astonishing emphasis.

"No, no." Olivia shook her dark head emphatically.

"Your mother is an especially *vulnerable*—" she hesitated "—no, you don't know that word."

"Yes, I do." Tali looked up for Olivia's approval. "It means sad."

"Kind of, yes—you're a clever girl."

"Because I read a lot." Tali's voice took on a proud note.

"Then you're assured of life-long enjoyment, Tali. People who don't enjoy reading are deprived. What I started to say is, your mother was somehow damaged by life when she was growing up. She's a person who has hurt other people but she was hurt herself, that's what makes life difficult for her. We must feel sorry for her, Tali. I'm sure in her own way she loves you."

"No, she doesn't," Tali contradicted flatly but not rudely. "It's all right, Livvy. I don't mind. Daddy loves me. Nona loves me. You love me and I love you so much. Danny loves me, too. He thinks I'm the smartest kid he knows. By the way he wants me to come over this afternoon. Can I? Just for a while. His mum can pick me up—she said so."

"I'll have a little word with his mother first," Olivia said.

"That's okay." Tali looked up at Olivia with a big smile. "They really like me over there. Mrs. Nelson's little boy Steven likes me, too. He's not as interesting as Danny and he can't do sums in his head like me. She's a nice lady, Mrs. Nelson and she's sweet on Daddy every time she sees him she goes pink. How did she get that scar on her face? She's still pretty."

"It was an accident, Tali. Don't mention it to Steven. It might upset him."

"Oh, I won't. It's just us two. Do you think Mr. Carlo will come and see me? I really liked his face and he spoke to me so nicely."

"He liked you, too, Tali," Olivia said quietly. "Carlo is his Christian name. His surname is De Luca. He comes from an Italian family."

"Like me," Tali said happily. "The best thing is he has lovely blue eyes like Daddy and a really nice voice. He's not as handsome as Daddy, though—no one is—but he's pretty nice all the same. Will you speak to Danny's mother now, Livvy? Danny's great at thinking up new games. I didn't like to ask you when my mother was here."

With a friend like Danny who needed mothers? Olivia lamented. Hand in hand with Tali she walked to the phone. It would be much easier to talk to Jason if Tali weren't around. She couldn't possibly let Jason go to a meeting with Carlo De Luca not knowing what lay in store for him.

Jason, my love! Her heart ached for the inescapable loss that surely confronted him for the *what might have been* for the two of them, the halcyon days they had surely enjoyed. It ached for her own gullibility. For Jason's decision to do the right thing to stand by damaged little Megan Duffy. It was all written. Seven years lost. But Tali graced their lives.

Except Tali was Carlo De Luca's child.

CHAPTER ELEVEN

THE phone rang. Olivia ran to it thinking it might be Jason. Instead it was Carlo's fiancée Leanne calling to thank her for a wonderful evening. She sounded happy and relaxed— obviously Carlo at that point hadn't confided in her. Olivia took other thank-you calls. agreeing to meet her friend Lucy for lunch in town on Wednesday.

"I was thrilled to see you and Jason on much better terms," Lucy confided. "Everyone is. That's a really cute little kid! How could Megan ever give her up? So much for motherly love! Anyway see you Wednesday, Livvy. Can't wait!"

When Jason hadn't returned by three o'clock Olivia started to worry. She'd worked out he'd be back by two at the latest. Had some problem cropped up? Had Megan at the last moment refused to go? Was she going to make one last attempt to get more money? Megan had toughened considerably over the years. Do I really know who I'm dealing with here? Olivia thought. It was possible Megan had a boyfriend in tow. A co-conspirator. It was a tense unhappy situation.

To her relief Jason drove up ten minutes later.

She ran down the steps to meet him. "I was so worried. Where did you get to?"

Jason got out of the car, tall wide shouldered, lean hipped, vibrantly handsome in a simple white T-shirt and jeans. "We had to pick up Megan's things first," he explained. "She wanted something to eat—that took the best part of an hour—then I dropped her at the bus terminal. She didn't want to spend extra money on a plane ticket. I waited for her to get on. By that time she was over a serious temper tantrum and down to the scowling sulks. Poor Megan! She's her own worst enemy. No matter what you do for her it's never enough.''

''I don't care as long as she never comes back.''

''Don't count on it,'' Jason said. ''If there's a good side to Megan I haven't seen it. Let's go inside, I could do with a long cold beer.'' He put his arm around her waist steering her towards the house. ''Where's Tali?''

She rested her head momentarily against his shoulder. ''She wanted to go over to Danny's place for a couple of hours. I said she could. Danny's sister picked her up. She seemed quite disappointed you weren't around.''

''Sometimes a crush can be a bit of an affliction,'' Jason said. ''I hope Tali's not going to spill the beans about her mother turning up.''

Olivia's smile was rueful. ''As this point in her young life spilling the beans is second nature to Tali. Other children clam up but Tali reveals all.''

''That's Nona,'' Jason sighed. ''Much as I love my grandmother I can't find a cure for her dramatic behaviour. Tali's picked it up.''

''You sit here in the cool,'' Olivia said when they arrived on the terrace. ''I'll get your drink. I might even join you. It's been quite a day.''

''You can say that again!'' Jason groaned loudly, pulling out a wicker chair and sinking into it. ''If Tali won't be home for another hour or two I'll just have to content myself with making love to you.'' He flashed her an all-encompassing glance. ''Do you realize how wonderful it was to fall asleep with my arms around you?''

She blushed at the seductive note in his voice. ''I didn't think we had much sleep, did we?''

''Call it a little shut-eye. It was the most truly joyous experiences of my life. I love you, Liv—your beautiful face, your beautiful body and above all your beautiful soul. Speaking of which—'' he suddenly sat up straight ''—there's something going on in your soul. What is it?''

For a moment her guard was down. Love and anguish for him showed in her eyes. "There's something we need to talk about, Jason.''

His blue eyes narrowed. "So serious! You're not going to tell me you're going to leave me again? Not after last night. You *couldn't!*''

"That's not it, Jason," she said. Tension showed in every line of her body.

"That's a relief! Then it's got to do with Tali?" He made a guess.

Olivia turned away. "I'll get you your drink then we can talk.''

"I think we better talk right away." Jason frowned. "What is it that's troubling you so deeply, Liv? You think there's going to be more upset for me? Let me reassure you, I'm never going to let anyone wreck our lives again." He stood up, drawing her into a protective embrace, resting his chin on the top of her dark silky hair.

"Oh, Jason!" The tears, unbidden, started to roll down her cheeks.

He drew back in consternation. "Is it so awful? Didn't I tell you the worst thing that could happen to us has already happened. You love me don't you?"

"I've never stopped loving you." She lifted her drowning eyes to him. "It's because I love you so much I dread to hurt you.''

"Liv, if I've got you and you've got me what else can harm us?''

There was no escape. She pressed a finger to his lips so he wouldn't interrupt her. "I wish I weren't the one to have to tell you this, Jason, but there's nobody else who can do it.''

"Then let it out!" His expression darkened. "Don't be afraid. I think I know what you're going to tell me anyway.'' In a flash of precognition he made the quantum leap. Maybe it was something in Olivia's frightened eyes. She just had that *look*. ''Tali may not be my daughter?'' Even as he said it he tried to push the thought away.

''I'm so sorry, Jason.'' Olivia's tone was low, elegiac.

''But I raised her!'' he cried, his face contorting in pain. ''I love her. I thought she had my blue eyes. What a fool! Nona told me once she didn't. Was she trying to warn me?'' He shook his head as if to clear it.

''Megan lied to you, Jason. She knew all along who Tali's father was. You didn't have sex with her that night— she finally confessed. I should have trusted you. I have to accept part of the blame for all this terrible mess.''

''Who *is* Tali's father?'' Jason's voice rasped.

''Think about the blue eyes.'' Olivia tried to get her voice under control. ''The uncanny blue eyes.'' She tightened her arms around him like a shield.

''Not De Luca,'' he said dully, all colour leaching out of his striking face.

''He recognised her at once.''

''As *you* did. You *knew*. Why have you waited until now to tell me?''

She took a deep breath, squaring her shoulders. ''Please don't condemn me, Jason. I couldn't think what to do. It's such an emotional dilemma. I knew the grief it would cause you. And Tali.''

''Yes, Tali,'' he said harshly, releasing her and turning away. ''Happy, happy Christmas. So don't stop, Liv. Go on. You're evidently a lot smarter than I am. Carlo recognised his daughter. Now he wants her. Is that right?''

Olivia gave him a look full of sympathy. ''Yes, Jason, he does. But can't you understand that?'' Her whole body was trembling at the betrayal in his eyes.

''So you *had* to tell me?''

''Yes.'' She pulled a tissue out of her pocket and wiped her eyes. ''Carlo wants us to meet. I couldn't let you walk into any meeting without knowing what was going to confront you.''

"I can always count on you, Liv,'' he said bitterly. ''Just out of curiosity how do *you* feel about this?'

"I don't know what you mean,'' she said, falteringly.

"Well, you wouldn't have to contend with a ready made step-daughter,'' he lashed out.

That wounded her deeply even though she knew he was going through hell. ''I'm going to forget you said that, Jason, though I don't know how you could have said it. Tali is the dearest child. I've found it very easy to take her into my heart. I feel devastated for *both* of you.''

"Well, I've known Tali a lot longer than you have,'' he retorted with uncharacteristic bitterness. ''I've reared her as my daughter. I won't accept she's not until I'm given positive proof. I don't want to see De Luca, either, until he has that proof.''

"And when he has it?'' Olivia asked in a kind of despair.

"I can't cope with that yet, Olivia,'' Jason said. ''Probably I'll never be able to cope with it. But Tali is the main concern in all this. How can she be uprooted? Doesn't he care?''

"He does care, Jason,'' Olivia said quietly. ''Carlo, too, was a victim. He was robbed of the early years of Tali's life. He missed her entry into the world. He missed her first steps, her first words. He loves her already. He's her father. He identified with her wholly. He recognized her on sight.''

"Tell me how?'' Jason's blue eyes were scornful of that.

"She's his flesh and blood,'' Olivia said simply.

"That's all that matters then, is it?'' he asked bitterly, looking so devastated Olivia was filled with compassion.

"I understand how you feel, Jason.'' She stared at him out of her black fringed eyes. ''I can see you feel I somehow betrayed you. I didn't. I recognised how painful the whole situation is. The one who betrayed you was Megan Duffy.''

"So now we know why she went away with so little.''

He gave a bleak laugh. "She was frightened to stay and face the music."

"I think she was most frightened of Bella De Luca."

"And Tali knows nothing?" Jason dropped his head into his hands.

"Need you ask?"

He looked up. "What time did you say she had to be back here?"

"Half past four." Olivia told him quietly, thinking the cost was going to be much higher than she thought.

Jason started down the steps, speaking as he went. "I'll pick her up and go home. I need time to think."

The most extraordinary aspect to what turned out to be a series of truly harrowing meetings and discussions that left Olivia utterly drained and Jason looking as though he was in the middle of a living nightmare was the way Tali took the whole business of her true paternity in her stride.

"Now I can have two daddies," she said excitedly, climbing onto Jason's knee. "It'll be fun. I'm your little girl and Carlo's little girl."

"I think you're missing what it all means, Tali," Jason told her gently. "It means you'll be going to live with Carlo and Leanne after they get married which is pretty soon. March, three short months." Six had been suggested for a gradual transition.

"Oh, I won't *live* with them," Tali said, shaking her head. "I'll live with you and Livvy. You're going to get married, too, aren't you? I'll be flower girl."

Olivia averted her head, staring out over the flood lit garden. Jason looked as though nothing could be further from his mind than getting married.

"Of course I'd like to go and stay with Carlo and Leanne," Tali informed them looking from Jason to Olivia then back again as if seeking their permission. "Carlo said he's going to buy a nice big house for us. He's going to buy books and CDs and videos and a bike. He thinks I'm smart enough to learn how to use a computer.''

"Lots of things to make you happy,'' Jason said, smoothing her curls. "How do you get on with Carlo's family? His mother and father and his sister, Gina?''

"Great!'' Tali couldn't have been more enthusiastic. "They're Italian just like me. Aunty Gina showed me pictures of herself when she was a little girl—it could have been me. It's really strange but Carlo's mama is a lot like Nona. She throws her hands around all the time. I like her. She started to cry when she saw me. I said, it's okay, it's okay. She said she'll never forgive my mother.''

"That makes two of us,'' Jason said.

"I think she's going to make it through this,'' Jason remarked much later, when Tali was tucked in bed and they were sitting in the starry cool of the loggia. "Children are hugely adaptable,'' he added with wry sadness.

"Thank goodness for that!'' Olivia breathed, thinking at the end of the day Tali mattered most. "The difficulty is she thinks she's going to live here, Jason,'' she added quietly.

"She has a family now, Liv,'' Jason said, trying to focus on that all important point. "They're ready to love her.''

Olivia felt heartbroken for him. "They know what you've done for her, Jason,'' she said loyally. "They're not cruel people. They won't take her out of your life.''

"I don't give a damn what they do.'' Jason shrugged dejectedly and tossed back a stiff whiskey. "I had a daughter. Now I don't.''

"It sounds like you believe you won't have another?'' She was near to breaking point.

It must have sounded in her voice because Jason reacted swiftly. "Liv, darling, forgive me.'' Love for her cut through his anguish. He cherished Olivia. He couldn't have gotten through this nightmare without her. Jason went to her, going down on one knee before her. He stared into her face, the moonlight caught in her satin textured skin. "You couldn't have been more supportive when my mood has been so down. I've been taking that for granted. Forgive me, it's the shock and the most peculiar sense of disorientation. It's not the end of the world. It *can't* be. Tali is going to be okay, Carlo *is* her father, and blood binds them. Already he loves her and so does his family, Tali's family. I was the adoptive parent who got to look after her for a while."

Tears welled into Olivia's eyes. "You did a beautiful job, Jason. You took on the role of father and mother. Because of you Tali is a happy little girl. She'll continue to be a happy little girl, we'll all see to it."

"Yes." Jason murmured an agreement, thinking the pain would never pass. "We all love her. We just have to approach this extraordinary situation with Tali's best interests at heart. For a while, I guess, she'll have *two* families. Rather like a marriage breakup," he added wryly. "She'll stay with us. She'll stay with Carlo and Leanne. We'll all take care she's not shuttled back and forth. She's young enough to accept this situation without too much trauma I hope. Luckily she's got a fine feel for drama. I couldn't bear to see her unhappy."

"At least we know she took to Carlo on sight." Olivia tried to comfort him. "And he to her."

"The parental bond has swept everything else away," Jason mused. "It would have been too dreadful given Megan's abandonment if Carlo hadn't wanted her. Tali couldn't grow up knowing she had two parents so badly flawed."

"No." The word rose to Olivia's throat. "We have to think of future repercussions. A sense of *identity* is very important—Tali has to know who she is."

"While I have to play the stoic." Jason settled back into

the armchair beside her. "My duty seems pretty clear-cut. I have to return Tali to her rightful father."

Ever sensitive to his pain, Olivia gently touched his arm. "That won't stop her loving you, Jason, or you her. Tali told me she *actually* had two fathers—she seemed very proud of it...two grandmothers, a brand new grandfather called Salvatore—*Salvatore with the big tummy*—she has an aunt, cousins, handsome, vital people, all ready to love her. Carlo will never let her go. Any parent will understand that."

Jason's brow creased. "Understanding is one thing, acceptance takes time. I'm not *totally* unhappy letting Tali go to them. They *are* her family. They're in no way to blame. Megan caused all the traumas—she can't have a heart. Don't worry, Liv." He tried to smile. "I'll learn to live with this, just give me a little time. I can live with anything as long as I have you." He took Olivia's hands in his, kissing the tips of her fingers. "I want children, *our* children, that was the way it was meant to be, that was what we planned. Neither of us had much insight into what Megan was really like. Anyway, let's drop Megan, hopefully forever. I love *you*, Liv. How could you doubt it?"

Her eyes started to sting again. Olivia stood up abruptly, walking to the edge of the terrace and fixing her gaze on the glittering stars.

Jason came after her, turning her into his arms. "I *love you*!" He started to cover her face and throat with tender little kisses, tasting the salt of her tears. "I'm sorry I've been so angry. Forgive me."

"There's nothing to forgive, Jason." She reached up to stroke his cheek. "It's as Tali says it's going to be okay."

"Swear to me!" Jason looked intently into her eyes.

"We're pretty tough, aren't we?" Her smile quivered. "Despite all the unhappiness Megan caused us, we've survived."

"Survived, yes but the longing never went away, it kept

going on and on. Tell me we're going to get married very soon.'' Ardently he pressed her palm to his lips.

''Wouldn't you say it was about time?' she whispered.

The depth of feeling in that whisper pierced Jason's heart. ''You came back,'' he said, not holding back his own emotion. ''I was waiting. Harry, that canny chess player, moved us both into position. Harry, my friend, I mourn your passing.'' Jason tilted his head to the sky. ''Perhaps you're looking down on us. I believe you saw ahead to the fulfilment of a dream *our* dream.'' Jason looked back at Olivia. ''You were my first love, Liv,'' he said. ''You were the first girl I ever kissed. It would take a thousand years to forget you. You're the only woman I've ever loved or ever will love. We'll stay close to Tali. The De Luca's are good people and we'll work it out together. Life goes on…we share a destiny. Besides, we're going to have sixteen children of our own!''

For the first time in days Olivia burst out laughing. ''Sixteen?''

''You heard me.'' Jason suddenly swept her into a few breathless dance steps. Then he stopped, bending his head to her. ''Sixteen.'' He brushed his mouth over hers, the tip of his tongue tracing the tender contours. His strong arms cradled her back. ''I'll never let you up out of bed.''

The look in his eyes exhilarated her. Slowly she began to unbutton his shirt, peeled it back, inhaled his scent burying her nose against his chest, feeling the tickle of his pelt of hair. The thud of his strong, vibrant heart spoke to her.

Olivia, I beat for you!

It was all she needed.

She drew his hand to her breast, ever sensitive to his touch. ''Hadn't we better get started?''

''Oh, yes,'' he breathed, his voice full of fervent longing. ''With you beside me, Liv, I can make anything work.'' Hungrily he folded her into his arms, starting in to kissing her until she couldn't stand up anymore and there was nothing else for it but to carry her off to bed.

All human happiness revolves around love. Love is central to the bonds on which a family is built.

EPILOGUE

Two years later.
Tidings of Joy.
The christening of Baby Corey.

SUNLIGHT streamed through the tall stained glass windows of the church bathing the interior in a kaleidoscope of jewel colours. At the rear of the church, exquisitely decorated with mountains of pure white flowers, a small group of people formed a circle around the baptismal font of pearly, rose-veined marble, while the silver haired parish priest with his fine classic features performed the ritual of the holy sacrament of Baptism. The beautiful young mother of Baby Corey, her face as celestial as an angel's with joy, stood cradling her beloved child in her arms, her handsome husband, Baby Corey's father standing tall at her shoulder.

The god-parents were ranged around them, their expressions full of tenderness and the becoming gravity required of responsible Christian sponsors. Three sets of god-parents had been chosen. Tim and Lucy Calvert—Lucy being the baby's mother, Olivia's, oldest friend and chief bridesmaid at her wedding, Ben and Robyn Riley, recent newlyweds and Carlo and Leanne De Luca with Carlo's daughter, Tali, standing just in front of them, her father's hands lying with gentle restraint on her shoulders.

Tali was very excited, brimming over with pride. On this marvellous day she had so looked forward to she was all decked out in her christening finery, a lovely dress of white broderie anglaise Nona Renata had made for her, a big, blue satin ribbon atop her dark glossy mane which had grown

182

half way down her back. This was a very special day in Tali's life, the christening of baby Henry "Harry" Michael Alexander Corey with his floss of apricot-coloured hair and navy-blue eyes.

Harry was adorable. Tali had loved him from the moment Livvy had allowed her to hold him on her very first visit to the hospital after Harry had been born. Harry was her honorary cousin. She'd already told Livvy she would look after him. *Always.* She was so proud of him! Father Luke was pouring the baptismal water on his darling little head but he wasn't crying at all. In fact he seemed to like it, looking about not fuzzily like most babies, but *brightly* like a little bird. It was so funny Tali had to stifle a giggle.

Of course she would have been asked to be god-mother if she'd been old enough, only grown ups were allowed to be god-parents, Jason had told her that. Papa and Lee were the next best thing. She was an important member of her big family Tali thought with contentment, feeling the warmth and strength of her father's hands on her shoulders.

She'd been flower girl at Jason and Livvy's wedding. She had so wanted to be. It was a beautiful wedding on Havilah with lots and lots of photographs to treasure. She'd been flower girl for Papa and Lee when they were married a few months later. She had stayed with Jason and Livvy on Havilah while Papa and Lee were on their honeymoon in Bangkok. She was so *happy* she had so many people to love her.

Now little Harry! How lucky she would be to watch him growing up. Papa had bought a house not all that far from Havilah. He was a doctor at the hospital where Harry had been born. She hadn't wanted to go and live in Brisbane, she had *hated* the very idea. She *had* to be able to visit Jason and Livvy whenever she wanted so Papa said, *"Not to worry!"* he would come back home. Papa was very sweet. He didn't seem to notice Jason was still *secretly* her favourite. If Papa had said they had to live in Brisbane she would have run away, but Papa never made her sad and Lee was fun.

Back in Livvy's arms, Harry Michael Alexander was making little bubbly noises, waving his tiny hands like it was his turn to bless them all. Weren't babies the most adorable creatures in all the world! It was perfect Jason and Livvy had called their beautiful baby after Uncle Harry. Tali could still remember how nice Uncle Harry had been to her when she was little. Livvy told her it was Uncle Harry who'd brought her and Jason back together again. Because she was smart and growing up fast, Tali understood how Jason wasn't her *real* father—Papa was—but she loved Jason in just the same way because Jason was the father God had sent to look after her.

Nona Renata, dressed up to the nines was sitting a few feet away in a back pew. She said it was all so *dramatic!* Nona Renata loved drama She was a *tumultuous* person, Nona Isabella told her that and she should know! Nona Isabella wasn't much different. Tali could see Nona Renata had tears running down her cheeks. Of course they were tears of joy! Harry's christening was a beautiful moving service. Nona Renata had made Harry's lovely white silk christening robe as well as Tali's dress. Nona Renata was so clever!

It was a glorious day, blue and gold. The jacarandas in the church grounds were unbelievably beautiful so dense with blossom their canopies almost blocked out the sky. The ceremony over, they all walked to their cars to drive back to Havilah for a celebratory christening brunch which Godmother Robyn had insisted on preparing. Secure and happy in her second marriage to Ben Riley, a local planter, Robyn continued to carry on her successful catering business with the full approval and sometimes hands-on help of her husband who had taken on a new lease of life and the role of step-father to young Steven who was thrilled to be included in the christening party.

Tali ran to her father, tugging his hand. "Papa, may I ride back with Jason and Livvy? I expect Harry will want me to be there."

"Of course, darling." Carlo smiled down on his little daughter, watching her skip off. No-one, least of all him, had expected Tali to adjust so quickly and so cheerfully to the big turning point in her life. It would have been another story, of course, had he insisted on continuing his career in Brisbane, but he realized he had to make certain sacrifices and actually everything had turned out surprisingly well. He had slotted back easily into the community. His parents were ecstatic he had come home and he and Leanne had resumed their rewarding careers. Not that they all hadn't worked very hard to handle the emotionally fraught transition period as calmly as possible. Carlo would always be grateful to Jason and Olivia for the gentleness, the selflessness and the understanding they had shown. Carlo considered it a great honour he and Leanne, who had become good friends with Olivia, had been asked to be god-parents. It was an undertaking that had brought them all closer together.

"He's gorgeous, isn't he?"

"Yes, he is." Olivia smiled into Tali's enraptured little face. They were sitting in the back of the car with Jason driving.

"He's got Jason's red hair. I expect he'll have his beautiful blue eyes," Tali said fondly. "Petty, pet, pet, little pet!" Very very gently she stroked the baby's head. "Little peach! Peachy!" she crooned.

"We won't have to wait too long to find out," said Olivia, fascinated by her little son. She loved him so much it made her feel humble in the face of so much joy. She and Jason were ecstatic they had been granted their perfect, healthy boy.

"Of course he'll have my blue eyes," Jason assured them as though it couldn't be any other way. "I can tell he loves you, Tali."

Tali smiled radiantly. "It looks like it. He's got hold of my finger and he won't let it go. I'm going to take lots of photographs of him. May I?"

"Of course, sweetie," Olivia said matter-of-factly. "We must have lots of the two of you together."

"Oh, wonderful!" Tali's bright blue eyes sparkled with pleasure. She lifted Harry's tiny chubby hand and kissed it, savouring his lovely uniquely *baby* smell. "I'm going to have lots of children, you know," she informed them.

Olivia smiled at her tenderly. "I'm sure you'll make a wonderful mother, Tali."

"You know why?" Tali asked of them both, sounding miraculously happy and relaxed.

"Why, honey?" Jason glanced back briefly, turning into Havilah's long drive.

"Because," Tali answered. "*Family* is great!"

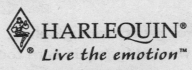

New York Times bestselling author Heather Graham choreographs a sexy thriller of passion and murder....

HEATHER GRAHAM

Accomplished dancer Lara Trudeau drops dead of a heart attack brought on by a lethal combination of booze and pills. To former private investigator Quinn O'Casey, it's a simple case of death by misadventure, but experience has taught him not to count on the obvious when it comes to murder. Going undercover as a dance student, Quinn discovers that everyone at Lara's studio had a reason to hate her—a woman as ruthless as she was talented. As a drama of broken hearts, shattered dreams and tangled motives unfolds, Quinn begins looking for a killer....

DEAD ON THE DANCE FLOOR

"Graham's tight plotting, her keen sense of when to reveal and when to tease...will keep fans turning the pages."
—*Publishers Weekly*
on *Picture Me Dead*

Available the first week of March 2004 wherever books are sold.